MEN
*in*
UNIFORM

# LILIAN
# DARCY

## PREGNANT AND PROTECTED

Published by Silhouette Books
**America's Publisher of Contemporary Romance**

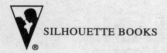

SILHOUETTE BOOKS

Recycling programs for this product may not exist in your area.

ISBN-13: 978-0-373-36297-4

PREGNANT AND PROTECTED

Copyright © 2002 by Melissa Benyon

Visit Silhouette Books at www.eHarlequin.com

**Printed in U.S.A.**

## LILIAN DARCY

has written nearly eighty books for Silhouette Romance, Silhouette Special Edition and Harlequin Medical Romance (Prescription Romance). Happily married, with four active children and a very patient cat, she enjoys keeping busy and could probably fill several more lifetimes with the things she likes to do—including cooking, gardening, quilting, drawing and traveling. She currently lives in Australia, but travels to the United States as often as possible to visit family. Lilian loves to hear from readers. You can write to her at P.O. Box 532, Jamison P.O., Macquarie ACT 2614, Australia, or email her at lilian@liliandarcy.com.

# Chapter 1

It only took a few seconds for Lauren Van Shuyler's whole world to change.

She heard a man's voice yelling, "Watch the crane. Watch the damned crane!"

Too late. Above her, the nineteenth-century brick façade she was here to inspect swayed forward, blocking out the light from a cool and drizzly late afternoon May sky. There was a clatter of falling bricks like gunfire, sporadic at first, then as dense as rain. The three-story façade toppled with the appearance of slow motion against the fretwork of scaffolding that outlined the structure of the new building going up behind it.

Several pieces of platform from the scaffolding spun through the air like playing cards.

"Back! Back! Back!" yelled the same man's voice.

Something heavy and warm rammed into Lauren, sending her to the ground. It—no, *he,* because it was a man's body—rolled on top of her, then pulled her with him, rolling once more. The movement dropped both of them onto their sides in a cold, narrow channel in the building's unfinished concrete floor, just a quarter second before several of the scaffolding platforms landed on top of them, followed by a thunderous dumping of bricks.

For at least a minute longer, Lauren expected death. The noise was like a bomb blast. The dust was choking, as dry and hard as chalk in her mouth and nose. The impact of the rain of bricks crushed and splintered the scaffolding platforms, which were acting as a bridge over the cramped space, shielding their two bodies. She felt a sharp stab of agony in her shin, followed by an oddly soothing spread of warmth, and then the gradual onset of numbness.

She couldn't move. The darkness was total, as thick and tactile as paint. She knew she was crying only because she could feel the way her chest was jerking, and knew the man lying beside her still lived only because the tight, fast shaking wasn't coming from her body, so it had to be coming from his. She'd never known such heart-hammering, gut-churning fear.

There was a roaring in her ears that deafened her to other sounds, and so many points of pain that she didn't know where to start counting. The roaring began to fade, and she could hear him—the man who was half crushed against her body—talking.

"Are you okay? Are you alive?"

"Yes. I'm alive." She gave several dry sobs like hiccups. "I'm alive."

"Good. That's good. That's one thing. That's one good thing." His body made one last jerky shudder, then was still.

"Is it finished?" Lauren asked. "The...the collapse?"

All she could feel now was his breathing, hard and slow and heavy against her body. She felt sick to her stomach, and wanted to cradle herself there with her arms, but she couldn't move them. One was stretched along the concrete channel, cold against its roughness. The other was pressed behind her, stretching the muscles tightly.

"I can't hear anything more falling. Can you move?" the man said.

"Not much."

"No. I guess not." His voice was deep and strong in his chest.

They both lay there for another minute, waiting and listening. Lauren's senses were in survival mode, alert and sizzling. She could feel cold air on her face, a thin breeze lazily winding its way along the channel. This suggested that it wasn't completely blocked at either end, and took away one of the most potent sources of panic. They weren't going to suffocate.

The air had the musty, limey smell of new cement, but there was plenty of it, and even the tiniest filtering of light, too, now that her eyes had adjusted. It must have come from the same distant source as the chilly stream of air, because it was weak and diffuse. The blackness had only shadings in it: midnight, charcoal, steel and storm. And she could see the faintest suggestions of shape. There was a smooth curve which had to be the man's shoulder, and a more blurred curve that must be the outline of his head.

Movement was almost impossible, however. Lauren was lying on her side, pressed length to length against the stranger. A piece of rough gravel beneath her hip bone made it throb with pain. The designer leather backpack she'd been wearing was squeezed between her lower back and the side of the concrete channel, forcing her spine to arch.

Splintered wood from the partially crushed sheets of scaffolding platform rasped her shoulder. She could feel one of the man's hands flattened beneath her rib cage. His knuckles must be grinding painfully into the gritty concrete. She had the impression, without much data to go on, that he was big. Her breasts were tender against the crush of his strong chest, and one of his thighs was lying across hers, heavy and solid and warm.

"Did—did you save my life?" Lauren asked him finally. She felt an instinctive need to get a fix on this new universe.

"That's a little too close to call, at this stage." His humor was edgy.

"I'm scared."

"Yeah...don't be, okay? Please, honey?" No one ever called her honey. No one would ever dare. But today, she liked it. It made her feel safe. "We'll do a lot better with this if we stay calm."

"I'm calm." But her teeth were chattering and she could feel the panic rising in her like the tide rising in an ocean rock pool.

"Cold?"

"I'm not dressed for this."

He laughed softly. "Atta girl! I didn't know there was a dress code for lying under a heap of bricks."

"I mean it, I'm not—I'm wearing a thin blouse." Silk. Expensive. Ruined. "I'm cold."

"Shh...bits of you are, yeah, but we're warm. Our core temperatures are warm. We're keepin' each other that way. We're okay."

His tone cajoled and soothed her, as if she were a nervous animal. If she stretched her neck back, she could see the faint outline of his face, rainy gray against a night gray background, and she could just make out his eyes. All of this was so close that it was only a blur. When she stopped trying to look at him and relaxed her neck muscles, her mouth or her forehead pressed against the soft cotton front of his shirt.

"My arm is going numb." Like her injured leg, but her leg was too far away to worry about.

"Let's try to move."

"How?"

"Planning and communication. The keys to any joint operation."

She tried to laugh, but the sounds were more like sobs. "How about some goal setting, too, while we're at it?" she managed to say.

"Good idea. Mine is mainly to get my fingers out from under your ribs. You have hard ribs, lady!"

"I…I've lost a little weight lately. And my name's Lauren."

"Ah, yeah, okay…don't apologize, Lauren. We wouldn't have fit in here at all if you were packing ten extra pounds."

"What's yours? Your name?"

"Lock."

"Lock," she echoed, tasting the short, masculine sound of it on her tongue. "Lock, can I move my arm?" It felt as cold and dead as marble. "And my backpack?"

"That's what I can feel with my fingertips? Leather, right?"

"Yes."

"Got anything useful in it? Food, or something to drink?"

"Some mineral water and a chocolate bar." She'd been a Girl Scout. She was—almost—always prepared.

"So I picked the right person to rescue, huh?"

"Only you didn't pick me. It all just—"

"No, I didn't pick you. Hell, yes, it was instinctive! I yelled at the others and rolled you into this duct cavity because you were the one I could reach. You and I were the ones right under that damned crane with its damned idiotic operator."

"You work on this site?"

"No, just visiting. Hell of a welcome, wouldn't you say?"

"I'd just arrived, too. I was looking for the foreman. Did—did everyone else get clear?"

"I don't know. A couple of 'em were clear already. A couple of 'em might have made it. Not everyone."

"No, I didn't think so."

They both listened again. No voices. No cries. No movement. There was a siren in the distance, but it must have been going somewhere else. Not enough time had passed yet, for help to have arrived. They both knew it would have to arrive soon.

"How long will it take them to get to us?" She didn't know why she was deferring to his judgment. Rationally, she knew that this experience had to be as jarring and new to him as it was to her, and there weren't many people in her life to whom she had to defer.

He took her question seriously, though. "We don't know how much stuff came down, how stable the site is, who else is under this."

"No. Of course. I'm sorry, I shouldn't expect you to have all the answers."

"It's okay. Hey, let's work on getting that chocolate."

They tackled it the way they'd agreed. Goal setting, planning and communication. First, they had to get his fingers out from under her ribs. Lauren felt them sliding around her side, coming to rest against her lower stomach. She heard him groan.

"I hope this isn't going to be worse," he said. "Can you reposition your arm now?"

"I think so." She scraped her elbow on the cement and the splintery wood, then realized aloud, "I don't know where to put it instead." She laughed, and there was a note of hysteria in the sound, which they both recognized.

"Hey, calm down," he soothed her. "Around my shoulder, okay?"

"Okay." It felt good there. His chambray shirt was soft, and the pad of muscle beneath it big and thick and warm. As feeling began to return, her arm tingled painfully but she rode it out without saying anything.

"Okay, now I'm going to try to get that backpack off of your shoulders."

"Please! Tell me what you need me to do."

It took several minutes of pain and effort, and the intimate contact of their bodies. At one point, his face was pressed hard between her breasts, which were unusually full and tender right now. A minute later, she had to shimmy her hips against his to make an essential change of position, and she could sense his sudden tension as she brushed against his groin.

Touching each other didn't feel wrong or bad, though. There were moments, in fact, where it felt like the only proof that they were both alive. Warmth, pressure, breath, the vibration of a human voice. Lauren hadn't felt such an urgent need for physical contact in a long time.

Finally, when she had to push her face into his chest so he had room to unwrap the chocolate bar, she found herself thinking, *This is good. Let's stay like this. I don't want the chocolate. I don't want to move.*

His shirt, and the smooth skin beneath it, smelled good. Safe. Beyond the lingering odor of brick dust, she detected a soapy scent with a masculine flavor. Sandalwood, maybe, and pine. It was fresh and somehow reassuring. Finally, although it didn't seem logical, there came an unmistakable nuance of applesauce.

"Got it!" he said.

"I'm thirsty. We should have gotten the water out first."

"You'll be thirstier after the chocolate. We should save the water until after we've eaten."

"Yes, you're right."

Her stomach and her taste buds still didn't respond to the idea of chocolate at all. She heard the brittle, low-pitched snap of the bar breaking and smelled the sweetness of it without appetite.

"Here," he said. "I'm sorry, Lauren. Clumsy. There's no choice."

She felt him cram the bar awkwardly into her mouth. A big, calloused thumb brushed her bottom lip, its texture rough in contrast to the silky chocolate already melting on her tongue. The flavor was too strong and rich and sudden. Why had she dropped the bar into her bag this morning? Why hadn't she chosen a packet of chips instead?

She managed to swallow the thick, sticky sweetness, but it seemed to cling to her throat. Her stomach heaved suddenly, a potent reminder of her new vulnerability in so many areas. She wasn't accustomed to feeling vulnerable. Not consciously anyhow.

"I'm sorry," she gasped, fighting it. "Water, Lock! Please!"

"Can't get to it." He apparently guessed what was about to happen. "You're not going to throw up, okay?" He barked the words like an order. "Breathe! Blow! Don't think about anything else. Just take a slow breath, then round your mouth and blow it out again. Steady. And then again."

She did it, desperately at first, then gradually with more control. *Breathe in, round your mouth and blow. Breathe in, round your mouth and blow. Yes. Yes.* It helped. It had worked. How had he known what to tell her?

"Thanks," she said.

"You okay?"

"I'm pregnant," she blurted abruptly, and started to shake. The adrenaline of finding herself alive and not alone had worn off now, leaving a deep inner chill of fear. "Dear God, I'm pregnant. What is this going to do to the baby?"

The panicky, tear-filled question was punctuated by the sound of sirens, faint at first, then whooping and keening as they gradually got louder and closer. Their shrill pitch was dulled by the thick blanket of bricks.

"How far along are you?" he asked against the rising crescendo of noise. "You don't feel pregnant."

"Five and a half weeks, the way doctors count it." She gripped his shirt, down near his waist. "I've only known for sure since the weekend. I don't want to lose my baby!"

"Shh, you won't lose it. You won't!" He managed to hold her. The pressure of his well-muscled arms was tight, awkward, yet intensely comforting. "It's tiny at five and a half weeks, just a bunch of growing cells, and so well protected in there, I promise. You didn't hurt your stomach. It's pressed right against mine. Are you having any cramping?"

"No. No, nothing like that."

"I promise you, little five-and-a-half week babies don't just jump ship because their mom had a little scare. Or even a big scare. It's growing away in there and it's doing just fine."

"How do you know?" she said harshly. "How can you possibly know? You're not a doctor, are you?"

The sirens were screaming now, and very close.

"No, but I've got kids of my own," he said. "Twin boys, not quite eighteen months. I *know*."

"Twins…" Her thought track ricocheted off his answer like a ball bouncing off a wall, changing direction abruptly. His answer explained the smell of applesauce on his shirt. "Your wife will be frantic."

"No, she died. A few months back."

"Oh, no. I'm so sorry. That must be terrible for you!"

"It's—yeah, it's okay." He sounded awkward, reluctant. Then he added on a rush, "It's been…pretty ugly. Guilt more than grief."

Lauren could tell from the harsh sound he made a second later that he'd let those last words slip without intending to. "Guilt more than grief." Just four words, but they betrayed a lot, and generated more questions than they answered. What did this man have to feel guilty about? Why couldn't he grieve?

She felt his struggle to move on, communicated by a tightening in his strong muscles, and knew the words were echoing in his head the way they echoed in hers.

"Uh, but, yeah," he said after a moment. "My mom—

she has the boys today—she'll be frantic when I don't show up."

"Dear God, help us…."

"This noise is for us now," he answered as the sirens began to die. "They're here. Listen."

"How will they know we're alive?"

"As soon as they turn off all those engines and sirens, I'm going to yell. I'm going to hold you tight and cover your ears with my arms, because it's going to be loud."

"I can yell, too."

"Then we'll just deafen each other. Let me do it. If I can stretch my neck back and get some more air in my lungs…"

But he yelled at bone-jarring volume for five minutes or more and there was no evidence that anyone had heard.

"There are some bends in this duct cavity, and concrete like this doesn't carry sound real well," he said finally, and then they heard the rattle of a broken brick falling a short distance away, and he took in a hiss of breath. "That's not good. If the sound waves from my voice were enough to shake this stuff loose… We don't know how stable it is."

"And neither does the rescue crew."

"No."

They listened, heard the sounds of machinery starting up. Being able to hear yet not to be heard suddenly plunged Lauren's sense of isolation to a frightening new depth.

"We could be here for a while," Lock said, confirming what she felt. "All night. Longer."

While they got colder and hungrier and their energy dropped and the wound in her crushed leg—which she hadn't yet told him about—got deeper. How much blood could a pregnant woman afford to lose? What happened if her temperature or her blood sugar dropped too low? She didn't know, and ignorance wasn't a feeling she liked.

She started to shake. "All night? No, that's too long! My baby…"

"Hey…hey…"

This time, however, the reassurance of that deep voice vibrating against her chest wasn't enough. Nowhere near enough to stop the tears, and nowhere near enough to stop the outpouring of words that followed, when at last she was calmer.

He managed to hold the water bottle to her lips and she drank. Then, cradled against him, she told him everything. Didn't care what words she used, or how they sounded. Didn't care that most of this she hadn't confessed before, even to her closest friends.

Why hadn't she? she briefly wondered. Why hadn't she told Corinne Alexander, for example?

Corinne had introduced her to Ben Deveson in the first place and regarded herself as his friend equally, so maybe that was why Lauren had said nothing to her. Nothing about the feeling she often had that this wasn't really *her*, engaged to Ben and pregnant with his child. Nothing about the feeling that there were two Laurens, one of them going through all the preparations involved in a big wedding, organized, excited and absorbed, while another Lauren watched it all in silence, screaming inside.

Which of those two Laurens was real?

Now, she asked that stark question to a complete stranger and didn't think twice about what she betrayed.

Who knew if she'd survive long enough to ever speak to another human being? This big, hard man with the tender, rumbling voice was here, and that was all that mattered. Bitter truths, extravagant regrets, dark fears. All of it was piled higgledy-piggledy in her heart and mind, and all of it came pouring out at random.

This was so ironic, this panic and terror of loss, because Ben didn't want the baby. And that was the part which hurt most. It had been haunting her all week, since she'd told him on the weekend just hours after taking the test.

With nothing to distract her inner vision, here in the darkness, Lauren could see her fiancé's face so clearly in her mind's eye that she felt almost as if she could reach out and touch it.

"And I must have known," she blurted to Lock. "At some level, subconsciously, I must have known Ben would react that way, because I didn't tell him when I first suspected. I only told him once I'd done the test and was sure. And then—"

She could remember his exact words.

"Good grief! How in the hell did you let that happen?" he'd said. "You told me you were using something."

"I know it's a little sooner than we planned—"

"Darn right it is! We talked about waiting three or four years, enjoying life first."

"It'll take some adjusting to, I guess, but... Oh, Ben, we've made a baby. Don't you think it's a miracle?"

Belatedly, he'd put on the right smile, the right voice, said the words—woodenly—that she'd hoped to hear from the beginning. Yes, it was a miracle. Yes, of course he was happy. It would simply take some getting used to. Plans were important. She ought to know that. But, yes, of course he was happy.

"And it was exactly the same tone," she said to the stranger, her voice muffled against his shirt and her breath heating his skin, "that he always uses when he tells me what a great time we've had in bed."

Only they didn't have a great time in bed, and she told Lock that, too. She told him how disappointing it always was for her, and that she hadn't felt ready to sleep with Ben in the first place.

"But, you know, we were getting pretty serious. It seemed like he had the right to expect it, especially once we were engaged. It was part of the package. I kept thinking it would get better. I mean, it will. It's my fault. I have to keep working on it. I should have realized that I didn't—" She broke off, then picked up jerkily, "No, of course I love him. He swept me off my feet. You know, he's not perfect. I mean, this is the real world."

That was something the silent, screaming Lauren didn't seem to understand.

"He's a good person, and— We're getting married in five days. I want to get married! I want a family. I *want* that. But how could he look at me that way when I told him I was having our baby? Oh, the baby!"

She moaned brokenly.

*Heaven above, how can I get her to stop this?* Daniel thought. *She's in some kind of shock. She's going to hate herself for saying it all.*

Every painful, heartrending word of it. He was sure of it because he already hated himself for those four little words he'd blurted to her earlier. "Guilt more than grief."

Dear Lord, how had they got to this point so fast, tapped into emotions like this so fast?

Lauren Van Shuyler had arrived on the building site, what, half an hour ago? An hour? He was no longer confident of his perception of time. He had seen her from the window of the portable site office, where he was looking over the plans for the new building's security system.

He'd known this was Lauren Van Shuyler, daughter and heir to the owner of the huge Van Shuyler home furnishings and hardware corporation. She was expected here to look over the construction of the company's newest store. Her visit had been planned for since last week, apparently, like a presidential photo opportunity.

Daniel had been curious about her and had manufactured a reason to go across to the site itself and get a closer look. His father had been her dad's platoon sergeant in Korea, and though the two men hadn't kept in close touch afterward, the connection was strong enough that John Van Shuyler had heard about Daniel's growing company and had sought it out to handle the security system for this new building.

Lauren had parked a low-slung, expensive car at the curb and picked her way nimbly and apparently quite cheerfully across the rough ground, which was rutted with the deep tread of a dozen heavy-duty tires. She'd looked cool and quietly beautiful in a dark red silk blouse and elegantly cut black trousers, setting off her rich, gleaming brown hair and fair skin. She'd worn a designer leather backpack, and someone had handed her a hard hat, although she'd never gotten around to putting it on.

Less than a minute later, that idiot up on the crane hadn't been looking where he was going, and Daniel had arrived just in time to roll her into this cavity and cement his father's old connection with her dad in a way no one would ever have wished for. His chest was pressed hard against two generous breasts, swollen and no doubt newly tender with her pregnancy. His thighs sandwiched hers. There was an uncomfortable feeling of fullness building just below his belt, which he devoutly hoped she hadn't noticed.

Lower down, he could feel a sticky moisture seeping through the fabric of his well-worn jeans and onto his calf. He suspected it was blood—*her* blood—but didn't want to say anything. She hadn't mentioned it. Maybe she didn't even know that she was injured.

She felt so good, smelled so good. There was silk and linen beneath his hands, and a scent like jasmine and orange blossom in his nostrils. Softness and warmth and femininity surrounded him, all close enough to breathe. How long was it since he'd been as close to a woman as this? Felt like a long time. That accounted for the fullness in his jeans. Becky had died just over four months ago, but they hadn't touched each other for months before that.

A man needed it. Missed it. The rough and tumble hugs he exchanged with his little boys just weren't the same. Kids, though…kids were pretty good. Yeah, he loved his boys, ached, suddenly, to have them know he was at least alive, although he didn't think Mom would even have heard about the building collapse yet.

Kids…

He kept thinking he'd like to get the fiancé, Ben, that this sweet-smelling woman was talking about hard up against a wall so he could yell a few home truths at the man.

*Jeez, buddy, you're engaged to her! You're getting married to her in less than a week. That's not how you react when she tells you she's pregnant. No matter how bad the timing is, what your doubts are, the first thing*

*you do is take her in your arms and make her feel good,
tell her you're happy, so she doesn't feel like she's the
only one it's happening to.*

*Even if, later on, your stomach starts caving in,
and your scalp is tight with anger and you're cursing
yourself for leaving the protection up to her...*

He could feel Lauren shaking. He would have
wrapped his arms around her more tightly to try to still
the convulsive movement of it, only it wasn't possible.
Their contact was already about as tight as it could
possibly get.

He didn't think she knew who he was, and wondered,
suddenly, if there'd been some self-protective instinct
at work when he'd told her his name was Lock. All
his friends called him that, and his closest professional
associates. Even his mother used the nickname oc-
casionally. Formally, however, he was Daniel Lachlan,
and that was a name Lauren would have recognized. She
would have known, then, that the son of her father's old
war comrade didn't grieve for his lost wife.

Daniel wished *he* didn't know half of what she was
telling him now about her own dark places. He ached for
the things she was saying. He would never have expected
a woman like this to possess such inner vulnerability.
Wouldn't have thought she'd know how to talk about it
this way, either. The stark honesty of her assessment
was devastating.

And she thought it was her own fault that she and her
fiancé weren't great in bed? That she was "too cerebral
in some areas"? From his current viewpoint, aware
of every soft, scented part of her, that seemed highly
unlikely.

"Honey, stop...*stop,*" he begged her, his voice
scratchy with tenderness.

"…and, you know, out of all of it, the only thing that really matters is not losing this baby. Dad doesn't even know yet. And he's wanted a grandbaby for so long…"

"Stop, please…let's not talk about any of this anymore."

"Please help me. I can't stop shaking."

"I know. I know, honey."

"Because I keep thinking, you know, that maybe Ben would…actually…be *pleased* if I lost—"

And suddenly there was only one thing Daniel could do to silence her. It didn't take much, either. He moved his mouth one inch down and half an inch forward and drowned the nakedness of her words in his kiss.

## *Chapter 2*

Lock's mouth was hard and warm on hers, and it tasted of brick dust and chocolate. Lauren gave a whimper of protest. She was engaged to Ben. She hadn't asked for this. She didn't want it. This man was a stranger.

But before she could pull her mouth away, or turn her head—and there wasn't much room in which to do either of those things—something changed.

Her convulsive shaking slowly ebbed away like water going off the boil. A sweetness flooded through her, an exultation that was primal and physical and somehow *necessary*. There was something vital about the touch of his mouth, about the imperious intensity of its pressure, and about her own instinct to respond.

Amid the barrenness of this concrete tomb and the starkness of her pain and fear, a kiss was like the first seed germinating on a bare slope of volcanic ash. It wasn't about sex or betrayal. It was purely about life.

The sound in her throat changed. It wasn't a protest anymore. It was a recognition. *Yes. Do this. Make me feel!* Not pain and discomfort, but something good.

Gradually, his lips softened and slowed. He let her breathe. She could have spoken if she'd wanted to. *Stop. Please don't.* Something like that. But she didn't say it. Instead, she waited for the moment, just a second later, when his mouth brushed hers again, and when the tip of his tongue parted the seam of her lips to gain entry.

They explored each other like travelers in an uncharted land. Without sight, Lauren's remaining senses were beginning to heighten their perception, and with such limited possibility of movement, all her focus was narrowed to their joined mouths. She felt his nose bump gently against her cheek and the soft nip of his teeth on her full lower lip.

His growing arousal was impossible to hide under these conditions, and she knew that her breasts, already heavy with their preparation for motherhood, had hardened into twin pebbles at their peaks. Inside her, low down, heat pooled.

It might have gone on for hours. Their imprisonment had begun to distort her perceptions now, and she didn't know how fast time was passing. Then the sound of machinery started to get louder and suddenly they heard the groan and grind of twisting metal quite close by.

Lock jerked his head back. Lauren heard it crack against the concrete two inches behind him, and she gasped as if she could feel the pain herself. She opened her eyes, couldn't remember when she'd closed them, but having them open made no difference. It was inky, velvety dark in here now. Night must have fallen outside.

"Your head," she said.

"I'm okay," Lock answered quickly. There was a slur and a creak in his voice, the legacy of that endless, motionless kiss. Were his lips as swollen and numbed as hers? "Listen, though…"

"I know. I can hear."

They heard a siren starting up.

"They must have found someone else."

They listened, frozen and silent, for several minutes. Lauren felt her body chilling down again. They were both damp from the heat of their awareness, and the fresh moisture had begun to cool. Her thin blouse clung to her like a fine layer of frost, and she started to shake once more.

She tilted her head down and pressed her forehead into his chest, needing the distance, although it was only a token. She felt the muscles of his arms tighten against her, sensed that he was searching for words, and simply waited until she found them.

"Look, I—" He stopped and tried again. "That was… unexpected. It wasn't planned."

"I know."

"It seems like we both needed it. To feel alive, or something."

"Yes, I was thinking exactly the same thing."

"Then you're not angry?"

"Was my mouth saying that, at any point?"

"No. Your mouth was…" he laughed suddenly "…the best thing I've tasted in a long time. It was…speaking poetry, I think. Singing it."

"A duet, then."

"Mmm." The sound rumbled in his big chest. "But now your forehead is plowing into my collarbone. That's not poetry. I thought you might be wishing it hadn't happened, or something."

"No," she answered. "Not that. But maybe I'm glad it stopped. I *am* glad," she added more firmly. "I'm having my fiancé's baby. I shouldn't be—" as Lock had done, she groped for the right words, for words of adequate power "—banqueting on another man's mouth, even if we don't—if we never make it—"

"We're going to make it, Lauren. We're going to get out of here. Listen to them!"

"What if they make a mistake?"

"They won't."

"The crane operator did."

"He was an idiot. In the site office I heard the foreman muttering about firing him."

"Pity the foreman didn't fire him last week!"

They both laughed edgily.

She said, "Tell me your name. Your whole name, Lock. I want to know who you are."

"No, honey, I'm not going to do that. I don't want you finding out anything more about me."

It was like getting a failing grade on a paper you thought deserved an A. And she was accustomed to scoring As in most areas of her life. All she could say, her voice tight, was, "Why?"

Daniel laughed again.

Ruefully.

He thought about everything they'd talked about before that kiss. Hours ago. He thought about her long, spilling confession. He thought about his own very brief yet far more damning betrayal. "Guilt more than grief." Becky didn't deserve to have anyone know that she'd gone to her grave insufficiently mourned by her own husband.

He sensed Lauren's hurt, but knew he wasn't going to rethink this.

"Because, sweetheart," he said, "when you wake up in a hospital bed tomorrow morning, you're going to be real sorry about a lot of the things you said to me tonight."

*Jeez Louise, that sounded harsh.* It was cowardly, too. Should he have admitted to his own regret as well?

To soften his words, he kissed the bit of her that his mouth could currently reach. It was her temple, where the skin was fine and where he could feel the downy edge of her hairline. He felt her move her head a little, and her answering kiss landed awkwardly on his jaw. He was so tempted...*so* tempted...to tilt his face down in search, once again, of something softer for his mouth.

He resisted it, and tried again. The words were better this time. Slower, more careful and considered. More honest, too. "People often do regret it, when they've spilled their soul to the wrong person. It can do damage. I'm sorry...about a couple of things I said to you tonight, too."

One thing. Maybe she'd forgotten it. He hoped she had. He waited.

*Don't bring it up again. Don't talk about it.*

"I won't be sorry," she said. "I needed to say all that to someone. About the baby, and all. I've been bottling it up inside me for a long time."

"About the baby, yes. Not the rest of it, honey."

"Tell me who you are."

"No, because I don't want tonight to be any worse for you—or for me—than it has to be, okay? I mean that. And when we get out of this, don't be surprised if I don't stick around."

"How could you not stick around? There will be paramedics and the rescue crew. They're going to want to know if you're hurt."

"I think you're the one who's hurt, sweetheart."

Ah, shoot! What was wrong with him? He hadn't wanted to tell her that! His mouth needed a safety catch on it tonight.

But it turned out she already knew. "You mean my leg?" she said, quite calm. "How could you tell?"

"I could feel something warm soaking into my jeans and getting sticky on my calf. I knew it had to be blood, and I didn't think it was mine. If you knew, too, why didn't you say anything?"

"No sense in getting you concerned," she answered. It was a quiet, matter-of-fact piece of courage that he had to admire. This woman was no lightweight socialite, living rich and easy on her father's success. It was common knowledge that John Van Shuyler intended to hand control of the family corporation over to her within the next five years. She would handle it well.

"It went numb pretty fast," she went on. "And there was nothing you could do. Now tell me your name."

"No. Let's talk about other stuff."

"Like what?"

"What's your favorite food?"

He felt her sigh. "Okay, we'll do it your way. My favorite food is split pea and ham soup, with lots of celery and carrot. My mother—she died about fifteen years ago—she used to make it on winter evenings, with hot biscuits on the side."

"I could do with something like that right now."

"Tell me yours."

"Favorite food? Anything that can't be mushed up and fed to a toddler!"

"That's perverse."

"No, because I've spent the last year with baby mush all over my clothes."

"I guess that makes sense."

"My real, serious favorite food is probably New York pizza, with mushrooms and onion, fresh out of the box."

Again, it seemed like hours that they lay talking like this. Favorite movie. Favorite season. Favorite moment in sport. Sometimes they agreed and sometimes they didn't, but it was the sharing and communication that mattered. Talking about things that existed in the light and air and warmth of the rest of the world made them keep on believing that the rest of the world was still out there. For both of them, it was necessary.

They heard more grinding, muffled shouting, silence. Then, after a long time, the faintest wash of pale light filtered into their vision, as if the far end of the duct cavity had been uncovered, and someone was shining a flashlight beam along it, somewhere beyond the bend. Lock yelled again, and this time someone heard.

"We're here, we're coming after you, buddy!" Oh, sweet life, the relief of hearing that human voice, a thin thread of connection to the rest of the world.

"There's two of us," he yelled back. "Lauren's hurt her leg."

They got questions and reassurance. Someone must have been assigned to them to keep up their morale, because it was always the same voice, belonging to a man named Kyle. Daniel answered, "Lock," when Kyle asked him his name. He described their position, and what he assumed had kept them safe—the bridge over this cavity, made by those sheets of platform.

"It won't be much longer," Kyle's faint voice promised them. "While you're waiting we're going to send you some warm air, okay?" A few moments later, Daniel began to feel the thin brushstrokes of air grow tepid and then warm.

"Watch the broken platform over our legs," he warned Kyle. "It's angled down, I think. Don't... uh...pull our legs out along with it."

He was pretty sure that a piece of the splintered wood was speared into Lauren's lower leg, but didn't want to spell that out too graphically in case he frightened her. Dear Lord, his need to protect her was surging in him like a physical force. To protect her from fear and pain and tragedy, and not just for tonight.

*Oh, jeez, I don't need this, and she doesn't need me.*

"We're starting the machinery again," Kyle warned. "I'm not going to be able to hear you. We'll take a break every few minutes to see how you're doing."

"Okay," Daniel yelled back. The machinery noise started up again, and above its volume he said to Lauren urgently, as if he might not have another chance, "Don't marry Ben. If it feels so wrong, don't do it. You won't be helping the baby that way. You can cancel the wedding, no matter how big and complicated it is. It doesn't matter about that."

He didn't know why he felt the need to speak. It was none of his business, not something he wanted to get involved in. Arrogant and presumptuous, wasn't it, to think he knew her heart like that? Why should he care that she was setting herself up for a miserable life? It was her choice.

None of which explained his emphatic repetition. "You have to cancel it. Don't marry him."

She didn't answer at first, and he felt her tension.

"You can't tell me something like that," she finally said.

"Why not?"

"It's not fair."

"After all the things you've told me about you and him tonight?"

"It's not fair," she repeated, and her voice broke a little. "I don't want to hear it. Not now, with the baby. I have to—I *want* to marry him. It's all slotted into place."

"Okay...okay."

She had started to shake again. Instinctively, he began to kiss her forehead and her hair, but she angled her head back.

"Please tell me who you are."

"No. No, Lauren."

"I can track you down." It was a threat, containing an odd mix of confidence and vulnerability.

Of course she could track him down, Daniel thought. With ease, since he was under contract to her father's corporation. She'd probably know his name as soon as she heard it. He felt the knowledge like a too-familiar emotional burden and fought it off, the way he should have been fighting off her effect on him all along.

"Would you?" he asked bluntly. "*Why* would you, if you knew I didn't want to see you again?"

He felt her stomach muscles tense as if blocking a punch in the gut, but her voice stayed steady. "I *would,* because I'm not going to let you make my emotional decisions for me, Lock. *I'm* the one who decides whether there's any regret about what I've said."

"And you want to decide the hard way, right?" He made it as brutal as he could. For her sake, for Becky's sake, for his boys, who didn't need people to know that he'd never truly loved their mother, and for himself. "By looking into my face and waiting to see if it feels like I've slapped you?"

Her breath hissed into her lungs. "Do you think I'm a coward, or something?"

"A coward?" He laughed. "After tonight?"

"Then stop trying to protect me from something I *don't need* protection from, and tell me your name!"

"No."

She was silent for a full minute before she said, "This isn't just about me, is it, Lock? I should have seen that before. You mentioned something earlier."

"I have other reasons," he admitted. Reluctance deepened his voice to a growl.

"Okay…" she said slowly. "Okay."

The next thing he knew, she had tilted her face to his once more and was ravaging his mouth with her sweet lips.

He kissed her back. Hell, he couldn't help it! She was so close. His arm lay against her lower stomach, and her hand rested on his shoulder. Her breasts were like two small, warm animals nestled into his chest. His fingers ached to stroke them through her blouse and bra—or maybe *not* through those silky fabrics; he knew her skin would feel even softer—to find out if they were as firm and full and giving as he imagined.

Instead, her mouth would have to do. Not exactly a deprivation, when it was so warm and sensitive.

Seconds later, there was a moist sound and a tiny sigh, which he felt on his upper lip, as she took her mouth away. "You already know who I am," she said. "That's the real problem, isn't it? I should have realized you would, if you were visiting the site. I wasn't thinking straight. Why didn't you tell me?"

"Why did you kiss me again?"

"Answer my question first."

He hesitated. "I was protecting you."

Was that the most important thing? Or was it the guilt? *His* guilt.

Guilt more than grief.

"Protecting me," Lauren echoed. "Just that?"

"Protecting myself," he admitted.

"Because you feel guilty that you didn't grieve for your wife."

"Yeah. Wouldn't you?"

"I don't know. I've never been in that situation."

"Trust me, there's guilt."

His eyes stung and he felt a terrible urge to tell her more, to babble it all out as if there was never going to be another chance in his whole life. Refusing to give in to it, he clamped his mouth shut so hard that he tasted blood on his lip.

Why had he felt this need to open up to a stranger, when he'd never acknowledged it to anyone else? Not to his mother, his older sister or his best friend. Mom still tiptoed around him as if his heart was buried in Becky's grave. He'd never admitted to Mom that he'd married Becky purely as a matter of honor, and he never would. It was a code of belief he'd inherited from his father. Real heroism lies not only in doing the right thing but in keeping quiet about it afterward.

There was more to it than that, however. He didn't want to admit to Mom how misguided he'd been to get involved with his office manager in the first place.

Hell, he'd known Becky was attracted to him from the beginning. He'd had that from the opposite sex since he was fifteen. That was when he'd shot up over six feet, his acne had cleared up, his physique had filled out and his sister Helen's giggling sixteen-year-old friends, with their thin veneer of maturity and sexuality, had suddenly found it impossible to behave naturally anywhere within fifty yards of him.

He hadn't understood it at fifteen, he'd blushed fire red every time, and he'd hated it. Even a couple of years later, when he understood it a whole lot better, he'd still hated it.

Since those teen years, he'd never been able to deal with women who were too blatantly interested. It turned him right off. Becky could have written the book on that kind of behavior and he hadn't responded to it at all.

Until Dad died.

Now, *that* was grief.

And Becky had been so…thoughtful, gentle, careful. She'd stopped her relentless flirting. She'd stopped engaging in transparent maneuvers to get him alone after everyone else had left for the day. Instead, she'd poured all her substantial energy and drive into genuinely anticipating his needs.

She'd gotten a little tipsy and tearful at a company party—he'd found it cute and out of character—and he'd had to drive her home and tuck her into bed. How he regretted what had happened next! Within a month, there had been a "mistake" and she was pregnant, just when he'd realized that the word *mistake* applied most of all to their whole relationship.

Guilt more than grief. He should have stuck to his initial instincts about Becky Gordon. He shouldn't have gone to bed with her. He shouldn't have let Dad's death cloud his judgment and make him so vulnerable…

"So you lied to me," Lauren finally said.

"I didn't."

"No?"

"I never lied. I just didn't tell you what I knew. About who you were."

"Or your full name."

"Or my name," he agreed. "Why did you kiss me again?"

"Because I have no regrets, and I wanted to prove it. That excuse is off the table, Lock. We're sticking to what's left."

He sighed. He wanted to tell her that things would look very different in the morning, in her nice bright private hospital room.

*You'll marry Ben, and you'll be miserable from day one. You'll watch an expensive divorce coming at you like a runaway train, and you'll hate me for hearing the truth from your own lips when you weren't prepared to listen to it yourself.*

"What's your name?" she repeated softly.

"Lock," he answered through gritted teeth. "I'm sorry, but it's still Lock. Do what you want, but you won't be able to say that I didn't try to keep this easy for both of us."

The machinery stopped. Lauren thought she could see some light filtering down from above. Of course the rescue team probably had the whole site floodlit to assist with their work. Kyle's voice pushed toward them along the duct cavity once more.

"Sorry about the noise, guys. We've almost reached you. You still okay?"

"We're okay," Lock answered.

"Lauren?"

"Yes, I'm here. I'm fine."

They started to feel the vibration of heavy machinery as the bricks above them were cleared away, then there was a shout and the sound of the engine diminished once more. Again, they heard Kyle's voice.

"Just the platforms now, Lauren, Lock. There are four of them, overlapping. We're going to take the last couple of 'em real gentle."

Time passed. It felt like around ten, maybe fifteen minutes. There was an earsplitting scraping sound right above their heads, and Lauren screwed up her eyes against the sudden glare of the work lights.

Her body from the knees down was still trapped beneath the final piece of splintered wood. She tried to open her eyes, but the light was blinding and right in her face. There were people surrounding them, uniformed rescue workers, paramedics. Voices came in a confusing sequence.

"Lock, we want to try to get you out first."

"We're going to cut away the last board around your legs, Lauren."

"Lauren, what can you move?"

"Not much," she gasped.

Lock was trying to climb out of the cavity but his limbs had stiffened in the cold, confined space and he needed help. Hands reached down. More questions came.

"Do you have any loss of feeling?"

"Can you try to drink this?"

Medical equipment appeared. More hands. Yet more questions. Lock was freed, staggering and crooked on his feet, which were about the only parts of him that she could see. The loss of his warmth immediately make Lauren start shaking again.

Her eyes were getting used to the bright light now. She opened them, looked for him, saw a broad, dusty, chambray-clad back that had to be his and tried to say his name, to thank him, or tell him not to go, but the words stuck hard and dry in her throat. Ambulance officers and rescue workers surrounded him. She tried to move her legs and felt pain ripping through one of them like a knife slicing through fresh bread. She almost fainted.

"We're going to need more tools," someone said.

Someone else had dropped a heated blanket over her and tucked pillows under her head and shoulders. A stethoscope dangled into her vision and she grabbed the arm that was reaching for the silver disk at the end of it.

"My baby," she said urgently. "I'm pregnant. Please don't let anything happen to my baby!"

Her words unleashed a new barrage of questions from the paramedic. She answered them as best she could, then heard raised voices from over where Lock was still standing.

"We have an ambulance for you, Lock. It's okay."

"I'm not hurt. I want to get home to my kids."

"We need to check you out first."

"Check me out here, then I'm getting home to my kids. My mom will be frantic. She didn't know I was visiting this site today. She won't have heard—"

"She needs a local in her leg and—" The new voice cut in over Lock's, and Lauren missed both sets of words. But then the new voice, the paramedic's voice, added directly to her, "I'm giving you a shot, okay?"

"Okay." She nodded. "Where?"

"In your leg. And I'm setting up an IV line in your hand."

"Go ahead."

"Are you current on your tetanus?"

She thought for a moment, then nodded. "Yes, I had one around two years ago."

"Your blood pressure and pulse are good, but we need to start antibiotics, and there's a mild sedative going in as well, because you might be here for a while longer if we can't get that leg out."

"Just do what you have to do."

And they did. It wasn't pretty.

*I'm going to faint,* Lauren thought again at one point, catching sight of her damaged leg. It was already sticky with blood and suddenly flooded with a fresh stream of it as a huge chunk of jagged wood was pulled from deep against the shattered bone. *Yes, I'm definitely going to faint....*

She closed her eyes, felt dreamy and distant from her own body, and realized that the sedative had kicked in. Wasn't sorry about it, either. The local anesthetic hadn't completely numbed the pain. She had questions about the collapse, about the fate of the rest of the building crew and a few other things, but those could wait. Or maybe they actually weren't important.

*Yes, these eyes are staying closed....*

She didn't open them again until she was lying on a gurney, being carried toward the waiting ambulance.

How late was it? Felt like midnight or later, but she wouldn't have been surprised to find it was only nine or ten. She considered asking someone, took a brief sidetrack into feeling glad that she hadn't worn her bracelet-style watch today to get twisted or scratched—it was a cherished gift from her late mother—and finally decided that opening her mouth and feeding language through it would be far too hard. Far...too...hard...

The lights were still white and bright, beaming over something that looked like the ruins of a Berlin building after the bombing in World War II. Piles of mortar-dusted bricks were etched with shadow. There was one section where the collapsed façade had landed like a draped blanket, with curves and folds that looked deceptively soft. There was a big dog on a leash, and someone going over the rubble with what had to be heat-sensing equipment.

At least one more person must still be in there.

Again, she wanted to ask the paramedics about it, tried harder this time, but something had happened to her voice. She opened her mouth and nothing came out. There was a clatter like a slow-moving freight car, and the gurney slid inside the ambulance and locked onto its metal track.

"All right, it's warm in here and we're going to get you on the road, Lauren," one of the paramedics said. "You take a little rest now, okay?"

"Mmm."

He took hold of the heavy rear door and began to swing it closed, and just before it curtained her vision of the scene, as if this was the end of a play's final act, she caught a glimpse of Lock.

It had to be Lock. That dust-drenched man with the stiffened, angular set to his big, handsome body, standing beside a late-model blue sedan with the door open and his keys in his hand, as if he'd forgotten what he had to do next. It had to be Lock.

*Why didn't you go in the ambulance? It's because of me, isn't it? You're doing everything you can to distance yourself from me.*

She hadn't said it aloud, and he couldn't have heard her from this distance even if she had. Still, at the exact moment her mind framed the silent question, he looked up, looked at the ambulance. The door banged shut, and she was left with a mental freeze-frame of his starkly lit face.

Dark hair, stiffened and gray with brick dust. Dark eyes, blurred at the edges by darker lashes. The mouth that had kissed her pulled into a tight line. A nose which looked as if it had withstood a few schoolyard punches in its time, and would be able to withstand a few more.

She would know that face when she saw it again, she knew. She would recognize him at once, when she defied what he wanted and tracked him down.

# Chapter 3

"Lauren, there's a printout for you in my office, but you can leave that until Monday. If you could just sign those letters on my desk though, before you leave?"

"Thanks, Eileen. You're heading off now?" Lauren didn't move her eyes from the computer screen in front of her. Figures filled it, and they threatened to start dancing beneath her tired gaze if she didn't will herself to concentrate. She'd arrived at five-thirty this morning, the day after Thanksgiving, and had barely left her office since.

"It's after six."

"Oh, my goodness! I'm sorry. You should have said something!" At last, she dragged her gaze away from the screen and frowned at Eileen.

"It's not a problem, Lauren." Eileen Harrap had worked for Lauren's father for over thirty years, and sometimes acted more like a loving aunt than Lauren's personal assistant, which she officially was. "See you Monday."

"Have a good weekend."

"You, too."

Eileen closed the door quietly, and Lauren turned back to the computer. She couldn't focus on the spreadsheet. Her injured leg was aching as it sometimes still did, even after six months of healing and extensive physical therapy. There were strange patches of light flashing behind her eyes. She buried her face in her palms, willing her vision to clear. Seconds later, the door opened again with a low-pitched click. She pulled her hands from her face, jerked around, straightened up and tried to look purposeful and businesslike.

It was only Eileen, but her face was a study in mixed emotions—apology, disapproval, understanding. "Did you remember you're eating at your dad's tonight?"

"Yes, I did."

"He's expecting you at seven."

"You got it."

"And the radio says traffic on I-95 is still pretty bad."

"I'll call him from the car if I'm going to be late."

Eileen looked as if she dearly wanted to say more, and once upon a time—six months ago, say—she would have done so. Now, although Lauren knew that Eileen's anxiety on her behalf ran much deeper, the older woman said a whole lot less about it out loud.

Many things had changed in Lauren's life in the past six months. She was more than seven months pregnant, and the baby had become a very real—and longed for—new being, close beneath her heart. There was no longer a large solitaire diamond engagement ring on her finger and no wedding ring, either. It hadn't taken long, after her rescue from the collapsed building, for her to realize that what Lock had urged her to do that night was right.

She'd told Ben from her hospital bed that their wedding was off. He hadn't taken it well. She was shocked at the insinuations and insults he'd resorted to. She'd never seen that side of Ben before. He had seemed unusually stressed and preoccupied that day also, and she soon knew why.

Just a few weeks later, he had left the country following the dramatic and very public collapse of his internet start-up company. He'd moved to Switzerland, preferring a luxurious exile to giving up the millions of dollars rightfully owed to the company's thousands of shareholders.

Lauren hadn't seen him since June, but his influence remained in her life. She was carrying his baby, although he hadn't yet committed himself as to what degree of involvement he wanted to have with their child.

She had also recently received some threatening letters. The wording wasn't very specific, but the meaning seemed pretty clear to her, and the police agreed. The letters came from one of Ben's disgruntled shareholders, looking for reparation.

"It's your responsibility, too. You must have been in on it," the first had read.

"Pay what's owed," said the second. "You can afford it."

"Pay willingly before you have to pay by force," threatened the third.

That was when her father had started talking about hiring extra protection for her, assessing her routine for danger points and retooling the security systems at corporate headquarters. Lauren agreed that it was a sensible idea, but she wasn't looking forward to it. Her pregnancy was making her tired, and she needed *more* privacy in her life right now, not less. The idea of having some corporate security consultant prowling around her home and asking questions did not remotely appeal to her.

She still had a lot of thinking to do before the baby arrived. Without the emotional trigger of getting caught beneath the collapsed building that day six months ago, she would have married Ben. The knowledge scared her. She'd come too darn close to making the biggest mistake of her life, and she wanted to guard against ever making such a mistake again.

If she only knew how to do that.

With a sigh, she closed the software program, shut down her computer and picked up her briefcase. She started thinking about what to take to her father's country house near Princeton, and whether she would accept his inevitable invitation to stay for the weekend.

She understood her father's concern, and wondered what he'd think if he knew that what preoccupied her more than her own safety was her memory of Lock. That night still seemed so vivid in her mind, and it nagged at her, lacking the closure she craved.

She couldn't forget the way Lock had felt, or the sound of his voice. She couldn't forget the things he'd said. And how he had read her situation with such accuracy. She remembered, too, what he had said about his wife.

Most of all, she couldn't forget the way they'd kissed. As if kissing was their only language. As if the touch of mouth on mouth was why their hearts kept beating. As if the world was coming to an end.

They had been buried alive together beneath those bricks for just under six hours, six months ago, and she hadn't seen him since. He'd been "a visitor" to the building site, she remembered. She'd sent a card there two weeks after the collapse, hoping it would reach him since it was addressed only to "Lock." Just nine simple words written inside. "I have no regrets. Please get in touch. Lauren." She'd wanted to tell him about Ben. She'd wanted to thank him, ask him why he'd been so sure. Yes, it was definitely about closure.

If he'd received the card, however, he hadn't replied.

She had hired a private investigator to track him down, but cancelled the man's contract before he could get to work on the case. That wasn't the impression she'd given to the few friends she'd told. They thought the detective hadn't managed to locate Lock, and that had stopped any awkward questions.

Even now, though, she could change her mind. She could pick up the phone, tell Gary Gregg of Gregg Investigations, "I do want to hire you, after all."

But she hadn't done it yet, and she knew that she wouldn't. Instead, she'd chosen to respect what Lock wanted and stayed out of his life. If he'd been so right about Ben, maybe he was right about this, too. But she was still thinking about him, far more than she wanted to.

Okay, the computer was off, she had her briefcase in hand. Surveying her spacious top-floor corner office, Lauren was nagged by the suspicion that there was something else, but her desk was clear and her desk calendar blank for the rest of the day.

"Get a grip," Lauren scolded herself as she left. "Or you'll have Dad offering headache pills and hot water bottles every five minutes."

She headed toward the elevator.

* * *

"That's Ms. Van Shuyler leaving her office."

"Man, she has a great pair of legs, don't she?"

Reaching the doorway of the security office in back of the main desk, Daniel gritted his teeth at the voyeuristic comments of the two guards on duty. He glanced at the bank of black-and-white security monitors built into the wall of the office, then looked quickly away again.

Yes, it was Lauren on the monitor, all right. It wasn't the first time he'd seen her over the past six months. Her father had employed Lachlan Security Systems extensively this year, and Daniel was currently overhauling the security for the entire building. That was fine. He'd only needed a couple of meetings with Lauren's father to talk about what was required, and on those occasions he'd managed to avoid encountering Lauren in person. He'd only seen her on these monitors.

Not for much longer. John Van Shuyler had a new proposition for him, in the wake of the threatening letters his daughter had received in recent weeks. The three of them were scheduled to talk about it on Monday afternoon.

Daniel was torn. Should he seek her out before the meeting with her father, put to rest the ghosts from that night, just the two of them in private? Or was it crazy of him to think that there were any ghosts to put to rest? Had she simply shrugged off those intimate hours together and forgotten all about them? She'd had a lot to deal with since their encounter. Maybe it was pure arrogance on his part to think that she ever thought about him at all.

It *was* arrogance. It had to be. And he didn't *want* her to remember their ordeal as vividly as he did. He wished he could forget it himself. Her strength and her vulnerability. Her laugh. The way she'd cried. What did they have to offer each other? Nothing.

*Leave it until Monday,* he decided. *Definitely. Leave it.*

Monitor 1 flashed silently to Camera 8, located in Elevator B, and there she was again. The gray of the picture and the odd angle reminded him of the way she'd looked as they lay in each other's arms. Neither of them had been able to see properly. Would she even recognize him when she saw him again? He didn't know.

The security guards continued their commentary to each other. They hadn't heard Daniel's arrival, and he still stood in the doorway with one hand resting against the jamb, lost in thought.

"Here she comes."

"Yeah, see what I mean with Camera 2? I'm definitely a leg man."

"Can it, guys," he growled, striding into the room at last, to collect his jacket and briefcase. He'd been working here for most of the day, but had had to put in an appearance for an hour at a product convention downtown.

"Wha—?"

Both men whipped around in their swivel chairs.

"I said *can* it," he repeated. "Checking out the boss's daughter is a good way to get yourselves fired, don't you think?"

"Yeah, okay, Mr. Lachlan."

"It was just a comment."

"I've heard she's a nice lady."

"Yeah, she is," Daniel agreed, distracted by the monitors again.

Lauren was crossing the lobby now. By the time

he gathered his jacket and put a couple of files in his briefcase, she would be through the revolving door and out of the building, and they'd see each other Monday, and it would be fine.

He was crazy to think anything else, after so long.

He picked up his things, said a quick good-night to the two guards and left. It was late, and he wanted to get home to his boys.

The letters. That's right. Eileen had wanted her to sign the letters.

Torn between a curse word and a sigh, Lauren chose a growl of fatigue and frustration between her teeth instead. She had to go back. Turning on her heel, she crossed the small plaza between the Van Shuyler building and the adjoining multilevel parking garage and pushed her way impatiently through the revolving door.

She saw a male figure in a dark, well-cut suit heading toward her, smack in the middle of her route to the bank of elevators and only about ten yards away. Even then, she was so unfocused she probably wouldn't have spared him a second look, only he stopped in his tracks when he saw her, and froze like a wild animal caught in a searchlight.

It caught her attention. It brought back memories.

Searchlights. Flood lights. A man's stark face and her own dazed stare. She knew that face and that body.

"Lock!" she said. "Good grief, Lock, what on earth are you doing here?"

She hurried toward him without taking a moment to rethink her reaction, stopped right in front of him, close enough to lay her fingers eagerly on his sleeve and look up, smiling, into his face. The draped front of her maternity dress almost brushed against his suit.

"Hi, Lauren," he growled.

"It's so good to see you! Were you looking for me?"

And then it hit her. Then, too late, she did what she knew how to do so well in business—she checked the situation out.

His body, in the masculine cut of the charcoal-gray suit, was as big and strong as she'd sensed it to be, and his eyes and hair were just as dark. His nose wasn't quite straight. He was incredibly good-looking, in a roughhewn way, as she'd somehow known he would be. But his body language didn't echo her own unthinking eagerness.

Instead, he was as close as a man could be to active recoil without actually taking a backward step. He looked horrified, guilty. And the conference nametag he wore on his lapel read, "Daniel Lachlan, Lachlan Security Systems."

Lauren had seen men in uniforms with the Lachlan Security Systems name and logo printed on it working around the building lately. She knew that her father had employed the company because of his old wartime connection with the company director's father. She also knew that she was scheduled to meet with Dad and Daniel Lachlan on Monday afternoon to discuss the issue of her own safety. What she hadn't known, all this time, was that Daniel Lachlan and the man who'd lain with her beneath the rubble were one and the same.

He'd known, though. Lock—Daniel—had known all along. All this time, he had been so close to her life that he could have reached out and touched her.

"I sent you a card," she said, only just managing to control her voice.

"I never got it."

"You said you were just visiting the site. I imagined you off in some routine that didn't connect with my life at all, and instead you've been spying on me via those brand-new, upgraded security monitors of yours."

"I haven't," he answered. "Really." He rubbed the back of his neck, and one shoulder rose uncomfortably. "I've caught glimpses of you, that's all."

"All? It's more than enough, isn't it?"

"Enough for what?"

"You knew I'd cancelled my wedding to Ben. You'd know that he's skipped the country, too. Dear Lord, you know *everything!* And yet it didn't occur to you—or more likely, I guess, you just didn't care—that I might need some resolution to that night. *You* were the one I spilled my guts to. *You* were the one—the only one—who told me, 'Don't marry him.' I respected what you wanted after that night, but I had no idea that your life was so close to mine. Instead I've been—"

She broke off, blinked back hot tears and was furious at her own betrayal. Doubly so because beneath her anger, all her senses had suddenly flooded with memories of the way his body had felt against hers. His heat, his weight, his taste, the pressure of his mouth on hers.

"—just clinging to that memory—" she kept going with difficulty "—because it was about the cleanest, neatest, simplest, most reassuring thing that's happened to me this year. That you cared about how I'd feel later on. That you told me not to marry Ben as if you cared. That you respected my privacy after the things I'd said. But all you were doing was protecting your own butt, wasn't it? Trying to hide from that guilt you talked about. Or was it the security consultancy? You didn't want to lose the work. Oh! This *stinks!*"

"Yeah, it does," he said at last in a low voice.

Lauren had pulled a tissue from her purse and was crushing it against her eyes. Daniel had a sinking sense, deep in his gut, that not making contact with her during the past six months had suddenly become one of the worst mistakes of his life. It hadn't felt that way before. It had felt necessary. The only thing he could have done. For his own sake and hers. Face-to-face with her, he understood that he'd been wrong.

"It does stink." He went on. "I knew we would be meeting up again, Lauren, but I didn't want it to be like this. Believe me, I didn't. I wasn't sure what that night meant to you. It's nothing to do with my work. I was just trying to give you some—"

He stopped, watched her shake her head, wheel around and stride back toward the revolving door. Beneath an open black leather coat, the beautifully cut gray wool maternity dress hugged her figure with a delicious emphasis that he tried to ignore. From behind, you wouldn't have known she was pregnant at all, and the security guards in their back office had been absolutely right about her legs.

"—space," he finished on a down beat, although he knew she wouldn't hear. He also knew that she was crying.

Well, good. Fine. She was right about most of it, wasn't she? Emotionally, he *had* been protecting his butt, and hiding from his guilt. Let her think that, let her deny him any other more honorable motivation, and let the buffer of her anger guard them from each other.

Guard? Why that?

He knew the answer. Because, to his deep dismay, the chemical heat they'd generated in each other that night hadn't gone away. Maybe it was the sensory deprivation of their entombment which engraved that kiss more strongly on his memory, or maybe it was the, yes, admit it, *voyeuristic* connotation of glimpsing her occasional image on those monitors, but Lauren Van Shuyler had slammed every one of his senses with hunger and desire the moment she'd touched his arm just now.

Ah, heck, it had nothing to do with the damn monitors! It was the six-hour press of her body against his, the six-hour jasmine-and-orange blossom scent of her, the sweet six-hour sound of her voice and its vibration against his rib cage, all of it still so vivid in his memory.

He didn't want that sort of chemistry. He'd been so wrong in his understanding of the woman he'd married. It would be a long time before he'd be ready to trust his own perceptions in that area again. On the other hand, when he stopped to think about it, he didn't want this anger and distance, either. Couldn't two intelligent adults manage to do better than this?

"Lauren!" he yelled after her.

She hadn't heard, or she wasn't listening.

The revolving door sighed to a stop behind her and she was lost to his sight in the darkness. All he could see was the reflection of his own big body moving awkwardly in the flawless mirror of the tinted glass. Let her go? No. If for no other reason, they had to meet formally next week, beneath the concerned regard of Lauren's own father.

They had to be civil to each other, and they had to find a way to tolerate each other's company while he fulfilled his brief regarding her safety. He couldn't let her go tonight in a state of such anger and emotion.

He pushed his shoulder to the huge door and sprinted after her. She'd almost reached the well-lit entrance to the parking garage, and her heels were echoing like gunshots on the paved plaza.

"Lauren!"

She didn't stop, but her pregnancy was slowing her down. Her pretty Italian shoes weren't designed for speed and his shoes were. He caught up to her just inside the entrance as her hand stretched out to the elevator button.

"Hey!" he said, and reached for her.

Big mistake.

She interpreted his urgency as aggression, and as he caught one of her hands before it touched the elevator control, she lifted the other and prepared to bring it hard against his cheek. With the security training he'd learned when he first started in this business, he was quicker. He snapped his grip around her wrist and ended up with both her hands in his, at eye level, her arms stretched to each side and her blue-eyed, red-rimmed gaze blazing into his face. He'd never seen her eyes up close before, never seen them in more than a blurred gray light. Despite the recent tears, they were beautiful, like exotic gems.

"Let me go," she said. Her chin was high and her jaw was square.

"You're wrong about my reasons!"

"I said let me go!"

He dropped her arms and she hugged them over the precious bulge of the baby, chafing her slim wrists as if he'd hurt them.

"And I said you're wrong about my reasons." It was much softer this time. "I'm sorry, Lauren."

*Had* he hurt her? Probably. In his haste, his grip had been rough. He reached out and tried to rub her wrists as well, but she shook her head. "I'm fine." She was still unconsciously protecting the baby, and there was something fierce and strong about her, despite the coexisting vulnerability.

"Listen, can we talk?" he said.

"We're meeting on Monday afternoon, aren't we?" She turned slightly to press the elevator button, but before her fingertip touched the panel, Daniel heard the machinery starting up, and the faint sound of the doors closing two floors above.

"It can't wait until then," he answered her. "What would your father think if he sensed how hostile you are?"

"He'd think that I don't want you working with me. Would you have a problem with that? Because it's a fact!"

"I'm not turning this contract down, Lauren. If your dad hadn't got my father to the field hospital when he did, Dad would have lost both his legs. My father never got a chance to repay that debt."

"You did, though," she answered. "You repaid it to me under a pile of bricks."

"I didn't do any more for you that night than you did for me. It went both ways, give and take, as needed. We took care of each other."

The elevator doors opened and a man in a blue jacket hurried out, glanced at Daniel briefly and loped through the exit out of sight. Neither he nor Lauren took any notice.

"If I can do it, if I can repay it," he went on, "by

watching out for you, finding ways to protect you from this creep who's threatening you, Lauren, I'm going to do that."

"I don't need you in my life, and you don't need me." She had her finger on the elevator button, keeping the door open. "You're the one who insisted on that six months ago, and if it was true then, it's truer than ever, now. I've got a baby coming and I'm on my own. Ben still hasn't indicated if he wants any involvement with his child. I've got lawyers already preparing to fight any claim for custody he might make. The last thing I want or need in my life is a man whom I'm supposed to get close to."

She stepped inside the elevator as if she thought the discussion was over, and he followed her because she was wrong. The discussion wasn't over at all.

"Are we talking about getting close here? I'm not looking for closeness," he said. "This is a job. Believe me, things are pretty complex at my end, too. We'll do what your father wants, then we'll close the book. That's all."

The elevator doors closed again, and she pressed the button for Level 3, where the executive parking spaces were, right beside the elevator shaft. Lachlan Security Systems would be putting extra cameras in that area next week.

"What my father *wants,* Lock—only I won't call you that, it's Daniel from now on—is for you to shadow my routine for at least a week and probably more, find out every detail about how I spend my time, where I go, who I'm with and whether it's safe. If you think that doesn't involve getting close, then you have a weird definition of the word!"

"Yeah, well, maybe I do," he shot back at her.

"Because close, to me, is what happened between us that night, and I promise you that's not on my agenda."

"Dad is just going to have to find someone else." She flung the words over her shoulder as she left the elevator, and once again Daniel followed her, not prepared to let the issue drop.

"He wants someone he can trust," he told her.

"And suddenly you own the only security company in the entire Philadelphia phone book that he can trust?" She wheeled around.

"He trusted Ben once, remember," Daniel told her bluntly. Was he hitting below the belt? He didn't care. "You both did. His trust for me crosses a whole generation and right now, with the concern he has for you, that's the only thing that counts for him. You won't convince him to hire someone else, Lauren."

Her eyes narrowed, and she gave a little nod. Clearly, she knew her father, and she knew that Daniel was right.

"Then I'll cancel the whole plan," she said. "The police are working on it. So far, they're not too concerned. There hasn't been a letter for a week."

"Fine," Daniel growled. "Fine. We'll see what your dad has to say about it on Monday."

"Fine. We will."

She turned once more, took her keys from her pocket and headed toward her car. Still watching her, his scalp tight with frustration, Daniel noticed the problem with her vehicle at the exact same moment that she did. He heard her gasp of shock, felt his heart thud in his chest and his stomach drop with a sickening lurch.

"Oh, my!" she stammered. "Oh, my Lord!"

She stumbled, and her hand stretched to support her

sapped strength against the cold white metal of the hood of her late-model BMW. It sat lower than usual. All four tires had been slashed.

## Chapter 4

"Now I'm mad!" Lauren said. "Now I am steaming!"

But she didn't look or sound angry. She sounded jittery, shaky and like she was trying far too hard not to be scared.

Levering herself up from her supporting lean on the car hood, she turned to Daniel and he saw the way her blue eyes glittered. Her lightly painted lips were shut tight. She had a gorgeous mouth, sensitive and full. He wasn't sure how she came to be in his arms seconds later—which of them had moved faster?—but he didn't dwell on the question, he just held her.

She smelled the same as the last time they'd done this. Jasmine and orange blossom. Hell, how could he have missed it so much, when he'd only known it for six hours? She felt different, though. Her pregnancy nudged his stomach, as hard as a basketball. Her breasts were ripe and full, heavy and soft.

*Just how unacceptable is it to find a pregnant woman this attractive? It isn't even your baby! Start thinking with something that resides above your waist. You need this woman in your life, you need this attraction to her, like you need a hole in the head. Don't give in to it!*

"This is a little nastier than a few letters, isn't it?" he said at last, lifting his jaw from its soft press against her cheek.

"And more expensive, and more trouble to deal with. I'm *mad!*" she repeated, and this time she sounded it. She let go of Daniel and straightened up, scrunched her pretty hands into fists and pushed one set of knuckles against the other. "Clearly this guy—this *person*—doesn't know me, or he'd realize that he can't get to me this way."

"I'm calling the police." Daniel pulled his cell phone from his pocket.

She nodded, her jutting chin dropping with a jerk. "Thanks. If I tried to talk to them right now…" She stopped and shook her head.

"You'd just splutter and hiss into the phone, right?"

"Something like that!"

He made the call. While they waited for the officers to show up, he drove his own car up to where her car was so she'd have somewhere to sit and keep warm. He knew without asking that she wouldn't want to go near her own vehicle. In any case, there could be fingerprints that she might smudge, though he was pretty sure there wouldn't be.

Next he called Lauren's father to cancel her planned dinner with him, and finally he called her regular garage and arranged to have them replace the tires and drive the car home for her once the police had finished with it.

The police didn't spend a lot of time at the scene, and Daniel wasn't surprised. They did their job, but a crime like this didn't rate against robbery, drugs and violence. The two uniformed officers weren't too impressed with his powers of recall, and he was disgusted with himself as well.

A blue jacket? A blue jacket was *it?*

They couldn't know for certain that the man who'd come out of the elevator while he and Lauren were involved in their…uh…discussion was the man who'd slashed her tires, but at least if Daniel had retained more facts, more details, the police would have had a chance of checking it out.

Just a blue jacket? No memory as to height or hair color? Age or build? Accessories, mannerisms or foot-wear? And Daniel was, excuse me, CEO of his own security consultancy?

The police officer who took their statements didn't voice his doubts aloud, but he didn't need to. It was all there in the way he looked at Daniel sideways from under his brows, and the way he laboriously noted his feeble description.

Even without his attitude, Daniel would have been burning, frustrated.

*I was so intent on Lauren, I didn't even take it in,* he kept thinking, when finally they could leave and he drove her home. *That's not how I was trained to be.*

She was quiet in the passenger seat beside him, drained by the whole thing, he guessed. Not mad anymore. He was the one who was mad now. At himself.

*That had to be the guy. I'm sure of it.* The thoughts ran on. At six-thirty on a Friday night, people came out of that parking garage on wheels, not on foot.

With his assistance to the police so limited, Daniel was forced to content himself with helping Lauren instead. He tried to hold her, once more, at the front door of her three-story executive town house. Her place was part of an elegant complex that strived for anonymity for its wealthy occupants, rather than ostentatious displays of luxury.

"This has been a rough night for you, Lauren." Damn it, even his words lacked any wisdom or power!

"I'm fine now. Thanks." She stiffened and he stepped back.

Was he relieved at her rejection? Or disappointed?

A mix, he decided, and one that was about as comfortable as five-course heartburn.

"Have you got food in the house?" he asked her.

"Plenty. Or I'll call out for something. I'm fine, Daniel," she repeated.

"Want me to come in?"

"No."

"I'm coming in anyhow, to check the place out."

She nodded reluctantly, her fair skin creased with fatigue and stress. It was unfair, he decided. Unfair to him, personally, as a man, that she still looked so beautiful.

"That makes sense, I guess," she said.

She stepped back and he brushed past her, aware once again of her scent and her warmth and hating his body for reacting this way.

*You have no time for this. You don't want it.*

"Do you mind if I don't shadow you while you're doing it?" she added.

No. He didn't mind.

He didn't make a thorough assessment—that was planned for next week—but he checked every room,

checked the locks on doors and windows. His impression
of the place taught him a lot more about Lauren in a
very short time. Less than he would need to know over
the next few weeks, but already enough to increase his
respect and his gut-level understanding, and more than
enough to make him uncomfortable. If he could, he
would have run a mile!

Her place was beautiful, every detail of comfort and
decor precisely thought out and perfectly executed.
Her antique-furnished bedroom was restful, her study
was efficient and her living room pretty, feminine
and inviting. In the granite and glass kitchen, she'd
summoned energy from some hidden corner of herself
and was actually cooking, making something that
involved pasta, basil and fresh vegetables.

The last room he checked was the new nursery for
her coming baby, and that just about tore his heart.

Although the baby's birth was still nearly two months
away, the room was complete and ready, from the brand-
new set of pastel bed linen in the custom-made crib to
the fat blue and white tube of diaper rash cream sitting
on the change table against the opposite wall. There
were children's books on the bookshelf, plush toys in
the crib and probably matched sets of infant T-shirts
and sleepsuits in the tallboy.

The impression it gave out was of a woman trying so
painfully hard to do it right, to stay on top of her life,
get ahead and keep control.

No, he revised immediately, Lauren didn't just want
to do it right, she wanted to make it perfect.

His mind flicked back to the stack of books he'd
noticed on the nightstand beside her bed. Pregnancy
books and child care manuals. Beside her TV there were
pregnancy exercise videos, and in the kitchen a neat set

of cookbooks featuring nutritional cuisine for young children and expectant moms.

*She's scared. She's so damned scared.*

This was why she seemed to be handling the threatening letters and the slashed tires with such outward strength, and almost disinterest, he realized. She was far too busy being petrified about something else.

*She lost her mother, what, fifteen years ago, didn't she?* he remembered, as he stood frozen in her perfect nursery. *And her baby has the* Forbes Magazine *version of a deadbeat dad hiding out with his money in Switzerland. She's got a fraction of the usual support new mothers need, and she's running scared, so she's decided she has to graduate summa cum laude in the motherhood course she's set herself, before the baby is even born.*

It was…sad and poignant and it said so much about the way she pushed herself, about how determined she was.

After he'd satisfied himself that she wasn't too easy a target for the disgruntled shareholder in her spacious town house, he stood by the phone while she called a friend to come and stay with her overnight. A couple of people were busy, and she had to make four calls. The smell of her meal cooking reached his nostrils as he waited for Corinne Alexander.

When she arrived, Corinne seemed eager to help. She was a glamorous, wire-thin blonde, making up in effort what she lacked in natural assets.

"This is just *insane* what's happening to you, honey!" she announced.

Daniel remembered that he'd called Lauren "honey" too, six months ago under the rubble. The sweet endearment didn't feel right to him anymore. It felt patronizing, and he didn't like the sound of it, coming from Lauren's friend.

"Totally insane!" Corinne was saying. "I'm so glad I can be here for you. And I'll tell you about my vacation in Europe. I had the best time!"

She wrapped Lauren in a tight hug, then turned to Daniel. "You're with security, right? Hi!" She didn't meet his eyes, and took no further notice of him at all. "What can I do for you, honey? Run you a bath?"

"I'm fine, Corinne," Lauren answered gently, as if she was soothing her. The carer, not the cared-for. "I just needed some company."

"Have you checked under the beds? Is your phone working?" Corinne was obviously the type who loved to be needed.

Daniel said quietly to Lauren, "I'll head off now, if that's all right."

"It's fine.

"And you'll go to your dad's in the morning?"

"Yes." Her nod was sharp, decisive.

Good. She wasn't just humoring him, he decided, and only then did he relax and switch his thoughts to his boys.

He was horribly late in picking up Corey and Jesse from his mother's. He was the person who minded most about that. Mom and the boys loved each other, but he felt as if he wasn't putting in the hours he'd like to at home. So maybe Lauren wasn't the only one who was taunted by unattainable visions of perfect parenthood.

"I have a very good head of personal security who could handle this assignment, John," Daniel said, leaning forward in one of the cream leather armchairs in Lauren's office.

He felt his suit stretch tight across his shoulder blades. The weekend of doing children's activities had taken the edge off his tension regarding the whole thing, but it was back again now, as he sat with Lauren and her father.

"Since the company has grown," he went on, "I've largely moved out of that area myself, so his expertise will actually be more current than mine."

He expected at least a few seconds' pause for thought, but John Van Shuyler didn't hesitate.

"No, Daniel, I want you," he said. The lines around his mouth deepened. Gray-haired but still trim, he had to be over seventy by now. "Consult with your personal security guy by all means, but this is personal at my daughter's end, especially the attack on her car, and I want full personal attention from you at yours."

Lauren's father spoke with the decisive speech rhythms of a businessman on a tight schedule. He'd been tied up with something else earlier in the afternoon, and the three of them had begun their meeting an hour later than scheduled.

"All right, yes, I appreciate that, sir," Daniel answered him.

He flicked a glance across to Lauren and caught the almost imperceptible shrug of her shoulders.

*You tried,* it said.

She looked quiet and composed this afternoon, in another pretty yet professional maternity dress of navy blue. She was clearly tired, but not shaky and angry the way she'd been on Friday night when they'd first seen her car.

John glanced at his watch and announced, "I have another meeting to go to. Could you two work out a plan?"

"I've brought some notes," Daniel answered.

"And I want progress reports, Lock, because my daughter can be very, very stubborn when she wants to be!"

Weren't both men supposed to laugh at this line? Lauren wondered.

They didn't and her father left the room seconds later. As soon as the door closed behind him, she felt uncomfortable. She didn't want to be here, and Dad's use of Daniel's nickname hadn't helped, with its reminder of six months ago.

Something suddenly occurred to her.

"Does Dad know that you were involved in the building collapse? That you were trapped with me?"

Daniel looked at her across the open top of the briefcase he'd set on the coffee table, his dark eyes shaded by brows set in a serious line. His hair fell across his forehead. "He does now."

"Since when?"

"Since he first approached me about the issue of your safety, last week. I'd managed to keep it quiet until then, but at that point, it seemed like he should know."

"So he's known for days, and he's said nothing to me!" She shook her head, disgusted. "I'm starting to get real sick of this!"

"Sick of what?"

"Sick of being treated like—like—"

"Like a woman who's had anonymous threats and violence directed at her personal property, and who is more than seven months pregnant and living alone?"

"No! Sick of being treated like a child who doesn't get told things that concern her because other people have decided, without her knowledge or her input, that she's not...what? *Intelligent* enough? *Strong* enough?

Emotionally fit enough?...to handle it. That's going to stop right now, Daniel!"

Leading with her pregnant stomach, she pulled herself up from the deep embrace of the two-seater couch with some difficulty and glared at him.

"I'm serious," she said. "From now on, you inform me fully of every development. Anything you hear from the police. Anything you hear from my father—since I apparently can't trust him to tell me himself! Anything you find out and anything you plan to do. One step out of line on that, and I will no longer consider what your father owed to mine, what secrets and connections we exchanged beneath that rubble, or anything else. You'll be...what is it TV cops say?...off the case!"

"Well, that's good to know," he murmured.

She glared at him again. "I mean it!"

"And so do I. It's good to know."

"Why?" She still didn't trust him.

"Because it's information I need. Point one. You're not running scared. You've got enough fight in you to care about how this is handled. Point two, you want full information and full consultation every step of the way. Not everyone does, you know. Point three—"

He stopped. His expression changed.

She waited for a moment, then prompted, "Yes? What's point three?"

"Point three. What's the time?" He looked at his watch, which was quite plain, with a tarnished metal band. She guessed it had probably belonged to his late father. "A quarter till six. I'm supposed to pick up my kids, but we still have a lot to get through. Could we do it over dinner?"

"Out? With your boys?"

"No, it would work better at my place. We'll pick up

pizza. I'm sorry, I know it's not ideal, but I'm going to be putting in extra hours with you over the next week at least, and I kind of—"

"That's fine," she said quickly. "I understand. No problem."

He had a look on his face that she hadn't seen before, and she realized that even if Lock and his wife hadn't been happy, he truly loved his kids.

In the emotionally fraught time they'd spent together, she hadn't thought much about how he would be as a father, and suddenly she wanted to know. She was thinking a lot about parenthood at the moment, looking for guidance from any source she could find.

"You don't have to explain," she went on. "Of course you don't want to short-change your kids. Pizza at your place is fine. We don't want to rush through this, do we? Since we're doing it, we'll do it properly."

That was how she felt about the baby, although apparently Ben didn't share her attitude. The last time they'd spoken, he'd said he had "lawyers and people working on it," as if being a father was something you could hand over to the appropriate professionals.

It hurt.

She hadn't let it defeat her. In fact, she'd toughened up over the past couple of months, ready to be a mother *and* a father to this new life inside her. She'd hired some lawyers herself, in case she had a custody claim to deal with, down the road.

But underneath, Ben's deep betrayal of herself and their child *hurt*. How could she have been so wrong about him?

"Did you drive yourself here today?" Daniel asked, cutting across her train of thought.

"No, I took a cab." She met his newly alert glance

and flushed. "Yes, okay, I was nervous about the parking garage. Was that wrong?"

"No, not at all. Nerves aside, it was the right instinct. No matter how cool you are about this, I don't imagine you want to get ambushed by some angry, out-of-control shareholder demanding a payout."

She looked at him, saw his narrowed eyes and the severe set of his mouth. The look emphasized the strength of his bone structure and the solid jut of his jaw.

"I knew nothing about Ben's business activities," she told him, "nor about his plan to flee the country when his company's checks started bouncing. You believe that, don't you?"

"Of course I do! I'll check into Ben's business and personal affairs as soon as I can, in search of leads as to who could be behind this. I didn't expect you to have a list of suspects on hand, nor to investigate the matter yourself. You've been caught in the middle of this, and you're pregnant, and you're obviously not at all confident about—" He stopped, then continued, "Actually, I think you've shown a lot of courage. Let's go, shall we?"

She would have liked to have seen his face at that moment, but he'd already picked up his briefcase and turned toward the door. Even more, she'd have liked to hear the end of that unfinished sentence. What did he think he'd learned about her state of mind? Where did he think she lacked confidence?

Apparently, despite her insistence on openness, it wasn't something he intended to share.

Jesse and Corey were adorable.

At his mother's house, Daniel's boys greeted him

with big, open hugs after he'd scooped them up and propped one on each arm. As Daniel was in and out in the space of a few minutes, Lauren didn't get more than a brief impression of Margaret Lachlan. Chunky thighs in comfortable stretch pants, short gray hair, worn-away lipstick, rolled sleeves and lots of laugh lines.

Daniel introduced her as, "A client. John Van Shuyler's daughter, remember?"

Mrs. Lachlan nodded and smiled, taking Lauren's hands in hers. "My husband looked up to your father so much. They should have kept in closer contact, then we'd have been friends long before this. I'm sorry you're having such a difficult time right now."

"Having Daniel involved will help enormously," Lauren told her. Politeness, really. The kind of thing you had to say. As she spoke the words, however, they felt good. True.

In the car the boys sang for the first fifteen minutes, then pointed out every truck and bus and ambulance that went past for the rest of the trip. Lauren listened and nodded and said, "Uh-huh," and wondered whether she was talking to them in the right way. She hadn't had much to do with kids at all and wished there was a course for her to take, to make up for it.

When Daniel returned to the vehicle with two hot cardboard boxes, Corey and Jesse said, "Pizza, yeah!" and clapped their little hands together, and Lauren couldn't help turning to the backseat to watch them. They had the bluest eyes, the silkiest curly hair, light brown with streaks of blond and the most delightfully joyous laughter. They looked happy and well-fed and loved. Just loved.

The attractive suburban house was a mess. Lauren was a little shocked at first. What about safety? What about hygiene? She stood stiffly in the middle of the lounge room, rubbing her tired back, while the boys immediately dropped to their knees to play. Daniel took off his suit jacket, rolled up his shirtsleeves and got busy in the kitchen.

*Surely you couldn't bring up children in this casual way!*

But then she looked a little more closely and discovered childproof locks on many of the closets and drawers, bubblewrap padding on sharp corners of furniture and an absence of actual filth that reassured her. Actually, the mess was kind of nice, she decided cautiously, and it was made of nothing more sinister than spread-out toys and unfolded clothes fresh from the dryer, colorful scribbled drawings and piles of household papers.

Daniel ducked into the room and must have read her expression.

"Sorry." He waved his hand. "It's a bomb site, isn't it? Some days, I don't get to clean up. Some weeks, I guess."

"Can I help?"

"Clean up? Heck, no!"

He strode back into the kitchen and she followed him. "I meant…with the pizza."

"What's there to do? Just sit!" He slid the pizza boxes onto the table in a cozy dining nook, grabbed plates and glasses and napkins, swung the boys beneath his arms, one at a time, like footballs, and washed their hands and faces at the kitchen sink. Within two minutes, he had them strapped into their high chairs and they were all ready to eat.

During all this, Lauren just sat there and watched. There wasn't time or opportunity to offer her help, and he seemed to be so good at this, and so casual about it.

She was impressed. Jealous, even. She was already apprehensive about how she'd handle a baby on her own, was still grappling with issues like child care and role models. At least she had the practical stuff—the nursery, the paraphernalia—fully organized, which made her feel as if she was a couple of steps ahead, on top of things.

And she'd read about a dozen books on the whole subject. To be honest, however, she'd emerged from those feeling overwhelmed with information and anything but relaxed. So far, Daniel made it look easy.

"You don't have a housekeeper?" she asked. He could afford it, she knew. His company was doing very well, and this modern house, although not huge, was solidly built and well furnished.

"I tried that," he answered. "I didn't like it. Felt like an invasion of privacy."

"Gee, why do I know how that feels?"

He ignored the rebellious line and went on, "I prefer the mess. We have one of those superefficient cleaning services, in and out in an hour, once a week, to minimize dust bunnies and actual germs, and apart from that it's just us three guys, living the way we like."

"Three guys, huh?"

"Yeah, so you know it's only going to get worse as the years go by." He grinned at her. "Here, have a slice."

She took one and said carefully—no, be honest, *primly*— "Isn't there a case for, um, setting them a good example, though? You know, taking care of your own property, showing respect for other people's space."

He looked at her, his mouth tucked in at the corners. "Which book is that in?"

"Um, I can't remember." She flushed a little beneath

his amused gaze. "But how did you know I got it from——?"

"I saw the stack by your bed the other night."

"Right." Well, admittedly, the stack was hard to miss. "Are there any that you would particularly recommend?"

"Not until I'd read some of them."

Her mouth dropped open. "You haven't read *any?* You must have!" She was genuinely shocked, both at the fact of it and at his casual attitude.

"I tried a couple after Becky died," he conceded.

And he'd dropped the look of benign amusement, thank goodness. She took a large, absentminded mouthful of pizza and propped her chin on her free hand, ready to listen and learn.

"Had them beside the bed, just like you do. Two chapters of one, three chapters of another, and it was like a horror novel. I lay awake all night. Sweating, remorseful, confused and convinced I'd already blown it totally."

"You're kidding!"

"I'm exaggerating," he said. "But seriously, in the end I decided that people with my vivid imagination and professional talent for envisaging worst-case scenarios should stay away from child care books purely out of self-preservation. Now I fly by the seat of my pants. I'm a lot happier and so are they."

"Do you *know* that? That they're happier?"

She frowned at him and took another bite of pizza. The two boys had tomato sauce smeared all around their mouths, puddles of sweet, fizzy liquid spilled on their high-chair trays and cheeks fat with cheese and chewy dough. This was the meal from hell, according to her latest nutritional bible. Salt and fat oozing from every mouthful, and hardly a vitamin in sight. But for once she didn't let it bother her. It tasted so good!

"Well, I guess we could do a controlled experiment," Daniel said. "Separate them for three months, handle one according to the theories of Expert A and the other according to the theories of plain old me and see which of them then scores highest on a battery of personality and intelligence tests."

"You're joking."

"Yes. I'm joking."

"And you think I'm neurotic, obviously."

He leaned forward, reached across the table, touched the hand that still curved beneath her chin. The caress was light, brief and almost, yes, fatherly, but it sent a ripple of remembered awareness in a warm wave all down her arm. Her breath went jerky for several seconds.

"You're not neurotic," he said, capturing her frowning gaze with a steady look. "You're in a difficult situation, and this is the way you've reacted. Tell me, is that in character for you? To overcompensate?"

"I guess it is," she admitted, then shrugged. Did he claim to have a different and more effective magic bullet? She needed *something*.

"Can I tell you to relax a little, or is that out of line? I'm only doing it my way with the parenthood thing, I'm not claiming to have the answers."

Pity about that...

"Relax," she echoed, then smiled. "There's probably a book on that, right?"

He laughed. "That's it. If there isn't a book, maybe I should write one. Laugh, relax, enjoy it, do the best you can, love them. Just love them," he repeated softly.

"I do." She curved her arm across her stomach, eyes pricking with tears suddenly. "I do that part already."

"I get down!" said Corey, the one in the red sweater. The boys didn't look identical, but it was a close call. He wriggled and struggled in his chair.

"Go inna baff!" Jesse agreed, starting to wriggle as well, although his mouth was still full.

"They want their bath. Can I focus on this for a bit, then I'll tuck them into bed and we can get on with it?" Daniel said.

"I'll clear up," she offered.

He told her she didn't have to, of course, but she did it anyway. She had enough time to tidy the living-room floor as well, and crawled awkwardly around on all fours, putting blocks and trucks and wooden train tracks in blue plastic storage tubs. Was this the shape of things to come? Or would she have a nanny to do it?

Neither alternative seemed to fit how she felt. She didn't want to put her role in Dad's company on hold. He was looking to have her take over completely within the next few years. But she didn't want to kiss her baby bye-bye at dawn and night-night at dusk with no contact in between, either. As a sole parent, were those her only choices?

"They're on their way," Daniel announced when he came back in. "Corey's just about learned to climb out of his crib, so I've got cushions on the floor beside it now. Jesse's a little more relaxed. Any day now, though, I'm going to hear a thud and some ominous little footsteps coming down the hall. Shall we start?"

He flipped open his briefcase, and she couldn't help watching the efficient way he sorted papers. She saw some brochures outlining various alarm systems, and a legal pad covered in his scrawled handwriting.

"You don't have a laptop?" she asked.

"Tried one for a while," he said. "Decided that with my needs and the amount of running around I do, I actually spent more time taking precautions against it getting stolen than it saved me in work efficiency."

"Makes sense. Go through your notes for me."

"Sure. I've broken it down into several distinct issues."

They spent twenty minutes on it, both of them focused and more than happy to keep to the point. Again, his efficiency impressed and reassured her. There had to be some safety in the fact that neither of them wanted to get any closer to each other than they had to.

This wasn't how she'd felt six months ago, she remembered. Back then, after their shared danger, the things they'd said to each other, the sheer fact of their survival, she'd wanted more. Ongoing contact? Closure, at the very least. Now she felt differently.

*You didn't always get closure when you needed it. Sometimes you just got complications. The simplest thing to do, the* only *thing to do, is to fight the memory and attraction and keep this as cool as you can,* Lauren thought.

They were just about done when he pricked up his ears, broke off midsentence and listened. A second later, she heard it, too—a rattling sound coming from along the hall. Then came a thud, followed by those "ominous little footsteps" he'd mentioned earlier, and Corey arrived in the room.

His blue flannel pajama pants were falling down, his curly hair was tousled and he had a huge, proud smile on his face.

"I climbed out, Daddy!" he said happily. "I climbed *out!*"

He launched himself into Daniel's arms, and Daniel rocked him back onto the couch, laughing like Lauren had never seen him laugh before.

"Little guy, you have *no idea* that I'm not ecstatic about this, do you? You think I'm going to be so pleased and proud about this great new trick you've learned!"

"And you are, Daniel," Lauren told him, laughing too. His amusement was infectious, tickling deep into her own belly. "Don't try to deny it, because I can tell. You *are!*"

He looked at her across the top of his son's head, still grinning. "So shoot me for it! This is why I can't take those books by your bed too seriously."

"Tell me. I want to know."

"Because not only do my kids never react the way the books say they should, but I don't, either. I'm supposed to frown at him right now. But look at how proud of himself he is! He thinks he's done great." He squeezed his little son tightly again and kissed the top of his head. "Could you do it by the book?"

"No." She laughed some more. "No, Daniel, you're right. I couldn't."

"Corey, are you sleepy?"

"No!" Blue eyes twinkled.

"Well, hey, what do we do? If I put you back, you're going to c-l-i-m-b right o-u-t again, aren't you, buddy, and we'll have a big, ugly battle on our hands." He spelled the critical words in what Lauren suspected was a futile attempt to play down the whole thing.

"Should I go?" she offered, strangely reluctant to have him take her up on the idea.

"Maybe if I just sit him on the couch while we finish. It shouldn't take long."

"That's fine. It's your call."

Ten minutes later when they'd finished, Corey was asleep, one dimpled hand softly curled on Daniel's thigh and his head on a cushion. Something twisted in Lauren's heart as she watched the two of them, a yearning need that she couldn't shape into coherent thoughts, let alone words.

No matter how dangerous and impossible it was, she needed something from Daniel Lachlan, and she didn't even know what it was. Wisdom, perhaps. Almost a year as a single parent had taught him a lot, while she felt terrifyingly out of her depth and unable to trust that anything about this coming baby could possibly be simple.

Support and sharing—did she need that? Just thinking about it seemed like a recipe for disaster. She needed to deal with things, solve things, decide things independently, not with the crutch of someone else's help. Especially not someone like Daniel.

In view of all of this, what she said to him next was possibly the worst question she could have come up with. In hindsight, it seemed obvious, but by then it was too late. She'd already said it.

"How did...how did your wife die, Daniel? Was it sudden?"

Dear Lord, this wasn't keeping her distance or respecting his boundaries! She hadn't paused for thought at all.

She thought he flinched a little, and Corey murmured a dreamy sound.

"I'm sorry." She stacked his notes for him, her fingers like nervous birds. "Please don't answer that! I had no right to—"

"It's okay," he said, pinching his chin between thumb

and forefinger. "I mean, it gets kind of unnatural when people skirt around it."

"Yes, I felt like that about my mother's death," Lauren remembered aloud. "It was like people were pretending she never existed."

"It's horrible, isn't it? It's not what you want, when someone has been that important."

"I know."

"I try to talk to these little guys about her. Nice stuff, you know. We look at photos together. They point to Mommy in the pictures, and they say the word now. Mommy. One day, though, they'll have to know about what happened. It was—"

He stopped and shook his head.

"Sudden or not sudden doesn't really enter into it, it just shouldn't have happened. You see, she developed gestational diabetes during her pregnancy, and it didn't go away after the birth. That happens to some women. She was okay with it at first, but then she read this book—"

He gave a bitter laugh.

"Maybe that's why I have a problem with certain kinds of books!" he went on. "I like thrillers, because they don't pretend to have big answers. Anyways, she got this whole crazy idea that she could control her diabetes with diet and exercise. She started going to this nutty and dangerous alternative healing group." He scowled. "Never told me she'd stopped taking her insulin. I came home from work one day. The boys were asleep in their cribs. Becky was lying on the bathroom floor in a coma."

Lauren suppressed a hiss of shock.

"The paramedics were great. Just fantastic. But it was

too late. They couldn't pull her out of it." He shook his head. "And I'm still angry."

"With her?" Lauren's voice creaked and it was hard to get the words out.

"Yes. With her. With the book and the diet and the group. With myself. Hell, *why* did I let it slip to you that day about the guilt?"

"You don't have to tell me—"

"I do. I need to say it now. I'm just sorry that it has to be you who has to hear it, because it's uglier than I want it to be."

He raked his fingers back through his hair, then brought them forward again to massage the knots out of his temples. His forehead, above that twice-broken nose, was high and squarish, suggesting his intelligence, but it had more lines there than should have shown in a man of his age. She didn't have the right to touch him, but if she had, she would have wrapped her arms around him and shared his suffering.

"It's so obvious that it just shouldn't have happened. If I hadn't been so miserable in our marriage, if I wasn't already angry with her for getting pregnant in the first place. Because she admitted she did it on purpose! If I'd been trying harder, maybe she would have told me about the diet and about what she was doing. I should have known Becky wasn't taking her insulin!" He stopped abruptly, as if he'd put a time lock on his mouth. "So there you go. The bottom line. Yes, her death was sudden, and if there was any way that I could grieve instead of feeling guilty like this…"

Once more, he shook his head. Their eyes met, zapping electric awareness back and forth. His mouth dragged her gaze toward it like a magnet. The way his shirt fabric clung to the muscles of his arms and shoulders begged her to reach out and explore.

"I'm sorry," he said, ending the moment. "You don't deserve to have that dumped on you."

"You don't deserve it either, Daniel. You're wrong about the guilt. You can't save people from what they want to do. I've been through all that because of Ben."

"So you've said it to yourself, too? 'If I'd known. If I'd listened. If I'd tried.' You've said those things."

"Yes, I've said them. Of course I have! Why didn't he tell me his company was in trouble? Why did he run away? Well, I guess I can answer that. Greed. But is it the whole story?"

"Locks both of us away in a pretty lonely place sometimes, doesn't it?"

"That's a good way of putting it," she agreed.

They talked about it a little more, both of them using clumsy, difficult words that might not have made sense to anyone else.

Finally, Daniel said, "Well, we're done here for tonight, so…"

"Yes, I'll go."

"You're feeling safe at your place?"

"There's no indication that the guy knows where I live. The letters have all come through our corporate mailroom, and of course the tire thing happened at work." She glanced down at little Corey, who had burrowed farther onto his daddy's lap. "Don't get up," she told Daniel. "I'd hate to wake him. They're such great kids, Daniel. I'll see myself out."

"It's okay. He won't wake up now. I'll let you out and then lay him in his crib."

Carefully, he stood up, shifting the sleeping child to his shoulder. Lauren could hear the slow rhythm of

Corey's breathing, and his little cheek was pushed into a fat apple shape against Daniel's shirt. She lifted her hand and touched the soft baby curls, and Daniel smiled at her.

"Best sight in the world, isn't it? Makes up for all the mess."

Lauren couldn't speak, just nodded and followed him to his front door. It felt to her as if they were separated by an endless chasm. He was the last man in the world who'd want to get close to a woman who was pregnant with another man's child and dealing with so much baggage of her own.

# Chapter 5

"Nice gym."

Daniel's direct, assessing gaze took in the immaculate shine on the tinted glass at the front entrance, the manicured plantings of winter color and the dust-free sign that proclaimed this to be the Cedarwood Athletic Club.

"It has all the facilities I was looking for when I joined," Lauren said. "And I've since discovered it has a really nice prenatal exercise class as well."

"Good security?"

"Yes, you have to show your pass in the lobby, and it has a photo ID."

"Can you wait in the car a minute? I'd like to check something out."

"Sure."

She watched him as he loped up the steps and through the automatic doors. He wore tailored pants the color of beach sand and a dark, chunky sweater with an equally chunky jacket on top. The clothing emphasized the solid length of his legs and the broad strength of his shoulders.

This had been a lot easier than she'd expected, particularly after his emotional revelations to her last night. Maybe their talk had eased some kind of pressure in both of them. Maybe they had achieved a kind of closure to what had first connected them. She certainly felt better, with a more positive energy and zest for life, than she had in months. Normally, it was teeth-gritting determination that kept her going. Dealing with Daniel and her own personal tire slasher felt, today, like challenges she could handle.

She had begun to sense, as well, how important Daniel's work was to him. He was approaching this consultancy as he no doubt approached others, his mind stimulated by the task of problem solving.

Arriving at her office earlier in the afternoon, he hadn't wasted any time on chitchat. Instead, they'd gotten right down to business. She was used to that. She liked achieving set tasks, crossing items off lists, moving important files from "In" to "Out." The questions and answers that batted back and forth between them like tennis balls had steadied her and made her feel in control.

He was happy with the security systems and protocols at Van Shuyler corporate headquarters, and they'd arranged for her to drive several different company cars in a random rotation until the man who had slashed her tires was caught.

Now he was assessing her gym. She could see him through the tinted glass, standing at the front desk and talking to a smiling receptionist. The conversation was apparently satisfactory to both parties. The receptionist was nodding and pointing with increasing energy. She typed something into a computer, listened to Daniel intently, and finally handed something to him across the high desk. Lauren couldn't make out what it was.

He said something that earned another huge smile, then loped back toward the automatic doors with a zesty rhythm to his steps. But by the time he reached the anonymous-looking dark blue Van Shuyler company car and slid into the passenger seat, he was looking a lot more serious.

"I have a visitor's pass to check out the facilities," he drawled. "Aren't I lucky? Vanessa, at the desk, was delighted that I was planning to join up."

Lauren caught the point at once. "That's not good, is it?"

"No, it's not. I had to show a photo ID but basically I was polite and well-dressed and all she saw was a potential new member. I could have been anyone. Hey, maybe our tire slasher is a member of this club already."

"Don't make me stop coming here." The words fell from her mouth, heartfelt and defensive. "I really like my exercise class, and I've made a couple of good friends who are also due in late January. We're planning to keep in touch and have our babies play together."

"I'm not going to make you stop coming."

"Thank you!"

"Let's go in. You can show me the pool and where you take your class." As they went up the steps together, he added, "I'll talk to whoever handles security here and tell them you've had some problems. I'll check out their cameras and their incident response procedures. By the way, when we talk about this, you always refer

to 'the guy.' But I want you to consider that it could
be a woman, or a couple. They're clearly looking to
intimidate you, get to your conscience, maybe, so in my
opinion a scenario involving some kind of confrontation
is a possibility. Say, in the locker room at a point in your
routine where you're feeling vulnerable."

"You mean when I'm changing, or naked and just out
of the shower?"

"Yeah," Daniel agreed, hearing the way his voice
caught on the word.

Hell!

She ought to be able to say the word *naked,* for
mercy's sake, without his body going into full tactical
response! Standing at the front desk while Vanessa
indicated various facilities, he'd seen an aerobics class
hard at work and he'd immediately thought of Lauren
in her prepregnancy shape, dressed in one of those
stretchy, figure-hugging outfits. "Naked" was just one
step further, and his imagination had no trouble in
stretching the distance.

When was it going to stop? Last night should have
been more than enough to douse the flames. *Any*
reminder of how unhappy he and Becky had been
should have been enough to put him off the idea of a
new connection with a woman. Permanently.

Except that it hadn't worked that way. Lauren's
acceptance of what he'd said and the fact that she saw
some similarities to herself and Ben had been cleansing
somehow. He felt lighter today and fully engaged by the
issue of how to protect her.

The problem was, the more he saw of her routine,
the closer he got to the inescapable conclusion that she
didn't just need alarms and cameras and vigilance, she
needed *him.*

Or a bodyguard, basically. He had a platoon of them in his employment, available for just this sort of job. Full-time, part-time, temporary, permanent. Squat, dark and burly. Tall, willowy and blonde. He had staff for the job.

But he knew that if this was what he recommended, John Van Shuyler would immediately, and with check-book in hand, want *him*.

*So I'm resisting,* he thought to himself. *I don't want it. She doesn't want it. Am I doing my job properly?*

"This is the room where we have our class," Lauren said.

She pointed at the glass-walled aerobics studio, where the class he'd seen was still in progress. The best thing that could be said for it was that it didn't front onto the street or the parking lot, but anyone who got past Vanessa could have lobbed a brick at the glass or invaded the room in person.

Daniel was torn. Was he simply protecting Lauren against the kinds of things that had happened so far? Or did he have to consider a further escalating pattern of threat? And how much notice did he have to take of the fact that she basically didn't want him here at all?

He sighed. "Where do you usually go?"

"I'm sorry?"

"I mean, where do you stand in the class? Front? Back?"

She shook her head. "Anywhere I happen to fit, I guess. I hadn't thought about it."

"In future, steer clear of this side. Go as close as you can to that solid wall and avoid the glass. Don't hang around the locker rooms if the place is quiet. There's an outdoor pool, right?"

"Yes, you can see it through here, from the deck

of the café." She walked in that direction, and he followed her.

"Avoid the deck. Stick to the indoor pool. You don't want to make it too easy for someone to get to you and get away again without being intercepted on the way."

"I hate this."

"I know."

He sighed again, letting the air escape through the side of his mouth. He was tempted to lay it out on the table, letting her know that this wasn't the best protection he could offer her. But it was the only kind he knew she'd accept given her attitude.

"Try to vary the times you come here, and the places you park," he said instead. Halfheartedly. "It's—" he spread his hands "—obvious, all of it. You just have to learn to think this way."

"Great! Fun! Because it's not like I have any other new kind of thinking to learn about in my life right now!"

The sarcasm dripped from her mouth and she stalked through the open-plan café and out to the deck that overlooked the pool. Leaning her forearms on the wooden railing, she scowled down at the deserted area around the drained pool.

"To point out the obvious," she said. "This is closed for the winter. One less thing to worry about. Gee, that makes such a difference!"

Okay, time to say it.

"There's an alternative."

"There is?" She looked at him across the fine-boned shape of her shoulder, which was hidden beneath a knit sweater of wedgewood blue wool. She wasn't wearing a coat today.

"Round-the-clock personal protection," he said. "Me,

when possible. A roster of people on my staff, after hours."

"No. No!"

He shrugged in an offhand way, purely to deny his relief. "Your choice."

She looked at him steadily. "It wouldn't be Dad's choice, though, would it?"

"I expect not."

"So we won't tell him. I've got some good evidence that you can keep secrets when you want to."

Suddenly it wasn't good enough. Sure, they could present a united front and pretend to Lauren's father that they had this all under control, but John was the one who was right.

"Is this really a point in your life where you want to take chances?" he asked her.

"This guy—couple, whoever—isn't spooking me, Daniel. I'm angry more than anything else."

"What about the baby?"

"What *about* the baby?" Her face had hardened defensively. The look of defiance and toughness didn't belong there.

"What percentage of a risk are you prepared to take when it comes to the safety of your unborn child? Ten percent? Twenty? Do you drive with no seat belt? How much alcohol do you drink?"

"Zero risk. For mercy's sake, you know that! You'd have to, after the way I fell apart under that rubble six months ago, afraid I'd lose my child. Zero risk!"

"Well, I can't offer you that, not the way we're handling this at the moment. And isn't any threat to your safety equally a threat to your child's?"

"I can't think about this now!" She closed her eyes.

"You have to!"

"We'll finish the tour of my routine. You wanted to see my church, take another look at my town house. *Then* I'll think."

"Okay."

"I'm cold." She crossed her arms and began to rub her hands up and down the sleeves of the blue sweater, but he sensed that the chill was emotional rather than physical.

She drove to the church she normally attended, which was on the edge of a business district that, she admitted, was almost deserted on a Sunday. Daniel wasn't happy about it.

Neither was she. "Now I'm supposed to skip church!"

"Change. Stay with your dad in New Jersey and go to his."

"He's not there every weekend. He has a woman friend he's become close to who lives in New York. He spends a lot of time with her these days."

"Come to my church. The location is safer, and the parking lot is very public and adjacent to the building."

She didn't reply. It made him wonder at his own crazy impulse in making the suggestion. He was sure she wouldn't show up.

At her town house, she wasn't a whole lot more helpful. He described the alarm system he thought would work best and told her he could have it put in tomorrow. She agreed. He asked whether she kept any valuables here. Was there a safe? Did she have cash or jewelry in her file cabinet? She gave a sarcastic reply, asking how he knew that the tire slasher was planning to diversify into petty theft.

He refused to bite, just asked, "Do you keep your file cabinet locked?"

"Yes! See!"

Without even turning to look at the cabinet just behind her, she angled her body a little, stretched out a hand and gave an exaggerated tug on the handle of the pale gray metal cabinet's top drawer, obviously expecting to meet the resistance of the lock. Instead, however, the drawer slid smoothly open and she almost lost her balance.

Daniel caught her and set her on her feet. He felt the familiar quickening of his blood at her touch and her warmth. His body had an impressively short reaction time when it came to this woman. He was still standing too close to her, his gaze caught by the serious bow of her mouth and by the tendrils of fine, dark hair at the nape of her neck.

He remembered those. He'd first known them by touch and smell, six months ago.

She, on the other hand, seemed genuinely far more rattled by the open drawer than by the sensation of his hands on her shoulders. "That's weird!" she said. "I *do* keep it locked!"

"And where do you keep the keys?"

"One set on my key ring, and the other here in this little—" She broke off and stared at the small antique pewter jug, half-filled with paper clips, that sat on a shelf next to the cabinet. "They're not here."

"No, they're here." He reached behind her and picked them up off the shelf, right next to where the pewter jug had stood. His sleeve brushed her shoulder, and his heartbeat sped up a little more. "Did you toss them back in and miss?"

"If I did, I— No, I didn't, and I locked that drawer!"

She pivoted and paced the room, her hands clasped beneath her chin as she thought about it.

"It was about a week ago. I remember because the phone rang before I got the key to turn. It's stiff unless you push all the drawers in real tight. When I'd finished the call, I came back and made sure I'd done it properly. And I buried the keys under the paper clips. I actually don't keep any sensitive materials in here, but…"

She'd lost color, especially around her mouth, her pupils had widened, her breathing was fluttery and Daniel's first concern was suddenly no longer her personal safety or the security of her files but how much food she had in her stomach and whether she was going to pass out.

"I'm going to make us a meal," he said. "Then we'll go through this properly. You feel like someone has been in here?"

"I know it! Daniel, I *know* it! I can't tell if anything's missing yet, but someone *has* looked through these drawers."

"And you're mad, right?" he asked, knowing she wasn't. "You said before that you were mad about what was happening."

She lifted her chin, took a step closer and met his concerned regard head-on.

"No," she answered. "This time I'm scared!"

Maybe it was the unconscious appeal in her widened eyes. Or maybe it was their particular captivating shade of blue and the dark length of their lashes. Maybe it was the way her full lower lip was trembling. Whatever the reason—whatever the *excuse*—Daniel had to touch her.

The scant second he'd spent with his hands on her shoulders a minute ago, steadying her balance, was like tasting one shrimp when he'd come for the all-you-can-eat buffet. It just wasn't enough.

He wasn't sure that touching her would be enough, either, but it was a start. His fingers and palms slid over the soft weave of her wool sweater, crossed at the knobbed line of her spine and settled against the muscles of her back. His chin brushed across her hair, then he bent his head, seeking her lips.

Just one small kiss. Nothing more than that, he promised himself too late. Just for comfort, not for seduction.

It didn't work. She made a little sound in her throat. It might have started out as a protest, but by the time it was finished, it was anything but. She wanted this, too.

He softened his mouth and touched it gently to hers. Once, twice, three times. The spaces between each kiss blurred and he stopped counting. Stopped thinking. Stopped telling himself this was wrong.

It *couldn't* be wrong, could it? Not when it felt this good. Her hair was thick and silky and fragrant. Her mouth opened and her neck arched back. He was raining kisses into her willing mouth and she was drinking them in. The tight clutch of her hands on his sweater, just above his pants, was asking for more.

He gave her what she wanted.

Anchoring his hands on the hard mound of her pregnancy, loving it because it was part of her, he let his lips trail down, across her jaw and neck. The sweater's rounded neckline was loose and open, but not loose enough. His mouth couldn't reach beyond her collarbone, and yet he was aching to get to her breasts.

Hands or lips, it didn't matter. He just wanted to

touch her there, feel her ripeness and her warmth and her weight.

She was wearing a second garment beneath the sweater—something silky and stretchy and thin that hugged her swollen body snugly and rested on her shoulders with two fine straps. Running his hands over it, sandwiched between silk and fuzz, he found what he was looking for. Two full, pouting curves that jutted above the larger shape of her pregnancy and strained against a lacy bra that was getting much too small.

She shuddered when he touched her there and made a sound of need as he thumbed her sensitive nipples through the layers of fabric. They furled at once into hard peaks. Her head twisted back on her neck and her breathing came fast and shallow.

Awed by the evidence of her pleasure, he kept his hands where they were, touching, exploring. Bending forward, he nudged each bra strap with his lips, and the straps of that other wisp of clothing he didn't even have a name for, until they slid from her shoulders. Her fullness spilled into his hands, firm and silky and oh-so-sensitive.

"I want to protect you, Lauren," he whispered. "I want to look after you."

"No, just kiss me."

He kissed her and touched her for what felt like minutes. Kissed her mouth, her throat, the whisper-soft tendrils of hair just behind her ear. Touched her breasts, the fine skin of her back, the warm knobs of her shoulders. Her hands were anchored to his hips, holding him against her. He loved the blind need she showed. She wasn't thinking about this, she was simply living it, feeling it.

Her eyes were closed. If she could feel the throbbing

demand of his arousal against the side of her thigh, she didn't care. She wanted it. Her hands moved to cup his backside, claiming it, teasing him in the way she caressed the creases at the tops of his thighs.

Needing more, he bent his head and touched his lips to her earlobe, then whispered, "Take this sweater off. And this silky thing. Please. I want to see you. I want to touch you and taste you with nothing getting in the way."

The words broke the spell for both of them. She had already stepped back, crossed her arms and grabbed hold of the sweater's stretchy waistband, ready to pull it up and over her head as he'd begged her to do. Her eyes were open but they looked blurred. Her hair was all over the place.

In his imagination, he could already see how she would look—the tiny, fine-skinned creases where her arms met her torso, the ripe bulge of her pregnancy, the push and swell of her breasts in their loosened cradle of lace. He'd pull her bra off completely with one flick. He'd touch her again…

But then she froze, shook her head, dropped her hands and held the baby instead, defensively. One shoulder had slipped free of the sweater, and when he reached for it, it was to slide the soft knit back up, not to explore the revealed shape as he ached to do. She let him, then shook her head, ran her hands lightly over her breasts as if reliving his touch, then let them fall to her sides.

She was right. Damn it, she *was!*

"We don't need this, Daniel," she said. "You know it as well as I do. For some reason, our bodies think we do, but they're wrong."

"Why are they wrong?" He needed to hear it from her.

Maybe that would drum it into his head! His own pep talks and reasonings had been patently insufficient.

"Because building something real, something that matters, between the two of us right now would be like building a fifty-floor building on a swamp. I don't know where this baby stands with Ben. Nowhere, I suspect. I have to work out for myself what that's going to mean. I have this stalker, whoever he is. And you…you know how much stuff is going on inside you. We've got no foundations, either of us, for anything but a short-lived affair, and I won't do that to myself, or to the baby."

"Lauren—" he began.

But Lauren shook her head. She didn't want to hear an argument from him that she knew would be based purely on physical need. The need itself, unfortunately, was not in doubt. They both felt it, deceptively powerful, deceptively alluring with its promise of ecstasy and oblivion, and its memory of what they'd given each other six months ago. Who wouldn't want to follow through on the chemistry they seemed to generate together?

But she knew that too much of what they *should* feel was missing, and too much of what they *did* feel was suspect in its origins. Emotionally, they were both coming from the wrong place.

"If you're going to try to argue," she told him, "answer a few questions for yourself first."

"What questions?"

"How much do you trust my emotions? And how much do you trust your own?"

"Not one bit," he agreed. "I wasn't going to argue with you, Lauren."

He leaned back against the gray-blue wall of her study, supporting himself with shoulder blades and elbows, his fists pushed against his lower back and his hips thrust forward. She knew he'd been aroused a moment ago. Hard, eager. She'd felt it—sought it, even—and the knowledge of his male response had melted her inside. But his sweater hid the evidence, now, and no doubt it was ebbing rapidly.

"You're right. You don't need to say it. I'm not sure that I've got it in me to find, with another woman, the trust that I should have felt for Becky. To find all the things I should have given her and didn't. Just the thought of trying to generate all of that makes me tired."

"I can understand that," she answered. "When you've tried with someone and it hasn't worked, it does make you tired. It feels that way for me, too."

"You know, sometimes it would be easier, wouldn't it, if we were like some animals? If we could have lain together that night six months ago, joined our bodies and then gone our separate ways. Instead, we have this craving for it to *fit* somehow, for it to mean something. But you're right. It doesn't. It can't. And we can't accept that, which makes it awkward, and messy, since we have to spend time in each other's company. I'm sorry. I shouldn't have kissed you just now."

"No," she blurted out. "You shouldn't have kissed me six months ago."

"Not then, either," he agreed. "I won't do it again."

"Suits me!"

The harshness of his assessment as to what lay beneath their need for each other suited her, too, the way a cold shower might have suited her, or an antibiotic injection. Things like this were hard to appreciate at the time, but they paid off later on.

"You looked pale earlier," he went on. "Really white. I'm worried about the effect all this is having on you." He gestured at the gray file drawer, which still gaped open. To her suspicious eye, the contents looked messier than usual. "It's after six already. I have a meeting later on, so Mom's with the boys at my place tonight. Why don't I order in something to eat and we can reach a decision about the level of protection you need?"

She nodded silently, too drained to protest against any of it.

## Chapter 6

Daniel cooked steak after she nixed the idea of sending out for something.

"Right now, even the thought of getting food delivered, having a stranger come to the house, is spooking me," she confessed as she tossed a salad to accompany the meal. "I have to get over this! I *will* get over it!"

"Couldn't you stay with your dad?" Daniel set a couple of baked potatoes in the microwave.

She shook her head. "He worries about me so much, it would make both of us neurotic."

"A friend, then?"

"I'm trying to be more independent right now, not less. I hated having Corinne come over the other night. I felt so weak, the way she fussed over me as if I was sick."

"Her reaction was a little over the top."

"She means well. Our friendship has had its ups and

downs, but we've known each other a long time." Since junior high, when they'd both had braces on their teeth at the same time, and they'd hated it.

"Did you two spend the whole evening together?"

"Well, we ate, watched a—" She stopped, understanding what he meant. "If you're suggesting that *Corinne* went through my filing cabinet...!"

"Who went to bed first?"

"I did. I'm pregnant, remember? My batteries cut out at around nine o'clock. But, Daniel—"

"Who has been here since?"

"Dad came home with me Sunday night. Some friends of mine, Patrick and Catrina Callahan, dropped in to return some videos they'd borrowed. I have a cleaner who comes Mondays, but she's— No! Bridget O'Meara? She's a fifty-seven-year-old Irish widow!"

"Those are your choices, Lauren. Unless you have a smashed window or a broken lock you haven't noticed or told me about yet."

"I've been checking every door and window the moment I get in the house."

"Good!"

"I hate this!"

"You've mentioned that."

"Wouldn't you hate it?"

"Yes, but I'd try to react rationally, not emotionally."

She gave him an arctic glare, but he only smiled a little. "Keep fighting. That's good."

Ignoring him, she said, "Okay, *rationally,* I've realized there was someone else came in here on Monday, when I was at work. I had a new desk chair delivered." She touched a hand to her back, which was troubling her more as the baby grew. The new chair was supposed to help. "The guy was here for a while, Bridget said, unpacking it and adjusting it. She's an unstoppable force once she starts cleaning, and she just went on with her vacuuming. She might not have taken much notice of what he was doing. If you can fit a theory around that, I'd be happy to hear it!"

"It's a possibility," he agreed. "After we've eaten, you'd better check to see if anything's actually missing. And here's another point. Bridget has her own key, right?"

"Hard for her to get in otherwise, since I'm mostly not here."

"You'd better remind her to make sure she never leaves it lying around. I'll see that the locks are changed tomorrow."

She nodded, chewing on her lip, then went to set plates on the breakfast table in a corner of the spacious kitchen. She also found a cloth, linen napkins, silver napkin rings and crystal tumblers for the sparkling mineral water her dry mouth craved. She didn't notice the way Daniel was watching her until she'd set it all out.

"You must have really hated my place last night," he said.

"It makes such a difference for only a little effort," she claimed, her mouth set as neat as a closed purse. Then she collapsed into the nearest chair and ground her forehead into the heel of her hand. "If you want the truth, turning into Martha Stewart's more perfect cousin is what I do when I think I'm losing control."

"If *you* want the truth," he answered her gently, "I'd already figured that out."

"Oh."

Their eyes met, and a smile wandered around his

mouth for a moment. It drew a response against her will—a goofy, fuzzy sort of grin. It was…kind of nice… to have a man figure her out. In more than a year, Ben never had.

Then he shrugged. "Sorry. It can be a fairly common response when someone's had threats."

"Oh, I do so love being consigned to a stereotype!"

"The sarcasm, on the other hand, is quite unique." His eyes teased her even more than his words. She wanted to find some anger, but couldn't. "Keep it up, if it makes you feel stronger," he said. "And you're right, of course. Control is important."

"Sometimes I think control is killing me," she confessed, feeling very raw beneath his gaze. "When I manage to let go, it feels so much better. I liked your home, Daniel. I liked the bits of it that were out of control."

"So how about you give a share of your unwanted control to me, and then you'll still have something left over—some energy and some feelings—to give your baby when it's born."

The microwave pinged. The aroma of the steak in the skillet reached her nostrils and her mouth filled with watery anticipation. She felt weak with a hunger that was relentless at the moment. The baby was growing fast and needed the calories.

*He's right, I can't fight this on my own.*

"Okay." She nodded. "Okay, you win. We'll do this protection thing however you think it has to be done, as long as we stick to one rule."

"What's that?"

"When I want the bodyguards to wait outside, that's what they do."

"That's acceptable," he answered. "And you've made the right decision. I'm glad."

She couldn't help noticing that he looked anything but.

"I am never going to get used to this," Lauren declared.

Her heels clacked on the floor of the corridor outside the Van Shuyler Corporation's executive conference room, sending pain shooting through her at every step. Her feet hurt. Her head hurt. Her back hurt. Image or no image, she wasn't going to wear these shoes again until after she had the baby!

It was a Friday evening, just ten days before Christmas. The meeting had ended late. She had a business dinner starting in an hour and fifteen minutes, and she had Daniel, still skulking around the building like…like… well, like the man who had been hired to protect her and who was going to do his job if it killed him.

He wore one of his usual dark suits, an outfit nowhere near tame enough to detract from the raw masculinity of the body beneath. His shirt would split its seams if he threw a single punch. His back muscles would ripple like an ocean swell if he had to pull off the suit jacket to get physical.

But he looked as if he really, really didn't want to be here right now. He was grabbing a surreptitious glance at his watch, and pinching his chin between his thumb and forefinger. She knew the gesture by now.

Not in a mood to waste words, she asked him, "What's the matter?"

"I'm not supposed to be here still. Lisa was supposed to replace me at five, but she got held up at another job, where there was some trouble."

"Wasn't there anyone else?"

"You know I'm pretty picky about who I have working this detail."

"You mean *I'm* pretty picky. Spill it, Daniel. Where is it you need to be?"

Was it a meeting of his own? Or was he going to his mother's house to pick up his boys? Yes, it was his boys. She could tell by his face.

"I'm supposed to be taking Jesse and Corey for a drive to look at Christmas lights tonight," he said, confirming the way she'd read him. He hunched his shoulders and pushed his hands down into the pockets of his pants. "I promised them. I mean, at two years old, I could distract them, or whatever. They'd forget." He laughed suddenly. "Heck, I bought their own Christmas presents right in front of them last weekend, and they never even realized!"

"Really?" Could that be true? She wished she knew more about two-year-olds. Adorable two-year-olds like Daniel's sons.

"Yeah, it was very cute," he said. "But I don't want to set a precedent for cheating them like that. Mom's been telling them all day about seeing the lights tonight. I hate it when this happens! At times like this, being on your own is the pits!"

"Your mother—"

"Just called on my cell phone to remind me she's going out of town this weekend to see my sister in Virginia. She makes that drive a lot, but she doesn't like doing it too late."

"I'm sorry, Daniel. You could have just left."

He didn't answer. He didn't have to. It was three weeks since he'd intensified the level of his protection. She knew him well enough by now to know that he'd need a bigger emergency than Christmas lights to skimp on this job.

"We'll pick them up now," she suggested. "Then your mother can get away for her weekend. We'll fit in the lights before my dinner. You can drop me at the restaurant afterward, make sure it's okay, and then you've got a couple of hours to arrange for someone else to take me home."

"But you wanted to get home and change."

He knew this because it was on the schedule. She hated the schedule.

"I'm fine." Who needed functioning feet, anyway? The blisters would heal.

He looked at her, shoulders still hunched, frown still dark. Her fingers itched, suddenly, to smooth the frown away, to linger, explore, caress.

"Please don't argue," she said, and there was enough in her tone to convince him.

"Okay. Yeah, it works, doesn't it? Mom's already fed them. She has some streets by her place where people do a great job with their lights."

He was striding in the direction of the elevator as he spoke. She kept up with him, blisters, head, back and heavy belly all protesting.

"It won't take long," he said. "Maybe there'll even be time for you to—"

"I don't need to change." As long as this black-and-white dress didn't look as limp as it felt. Well, if she didn't have access to a mirror, she wouldn't know, would she?

Lauren hadn't looked at Christmas lights for years. She'd forgotten how magical it could be. The night was clear and cold, but the heating in Daniel's car wrapped her aching legs in warmth. Daniel had stopped at a gourmet food store a few minutes earlier. In the backseat, the boys had the crumbled remains of fresh-baked Christmas cookies squashed into their fists, and smears of sweet stuff around their mouths. The air in the car smelled of butter and cinnamon.

Daniel cruised slowly up and down the streets, saying, "Wow! Look at that house, guys! Do you see the sleigh? And the elves?"

The boys began to say, "Wow!" at frequent intervals, too, and laughed in excitement.

Lauren was tentative about her own input at first. She was here by accident. She didn't belong. But then Daniel took a break from pointing out Santas and Christmas trees and angels, and told her quietly, "Nice that it happened like this. It's good to have two people in the front seat. And Mom was able to get away just a little later than planned. Thanks, Lauren."

"That's...fine, Daniel."

She had to struggle to hide the sudden thickness in her voice. It had been nice to see Mrs. Lachlan again, and they'd exchanged a warm hug. Her pregnancy was making her emotional these days. She was glad it was dark in the car. Looking across at Daniel, she found he was focused once more on the street. She took the opportunity to watch him, feeling greedy about it. A little guilty, too, and hungry for the right to touch him, to feel as if she belonged.

Not in his life. She was heavy with another man's child, and she still didn't know what that was going to do to her future. But in his arms, oh, she definitely wanted to belong in his arms, even if it didn't last.

The dim reach of the streetlights chased shadows over his face. He had one hand positioned, very relaxed, on the top of the steering wheel while he pointed again. "Look, guys! Look at that great tree!"

He was as alert in showing his kids the best lights as he was in watching for threats to Lauren's safety, and she had begun to respond to this quality in him more strongly as each day passed. If she ever needed a man to lean on, Daniel wouldn't let her down.

It was tempting...so tempting...until her spirit rebelled.

*I need to handle this on my own.*

As a distraction, she asked him, "What are your Christmases like, Daniel?"

"Big!" He grinned. "Mom likes to put on the full show, plus all the extras, like what we're doing tonight."

"What we're doing tonight is nice."

"It is," he agreed. "I used to shrug it off a little, but since the boys were born, I've realized that this stuff is what knits it all together. Your outlook changes when you have kids."

"I guess."

"What about you?"

"I guess my outlook will change. I mean, that's what everyone says. I'm trying to have everything in place, you know, to minimize the shock. Or whatever it is. I'm scared of it."

"Hey, don't be. And I actually didn't mean your outlook, I meant how are your Christmases?"

"Oh. Right." She nodded. "They're quiet. Now. My mom was like yours, though. She loved every detail."

"You miss it?"

"Well, you know, it's a big effort, and—" She stopped. Took a breath. "Yes. I miss it."

The boys had gotten quiet, and her business dinner

was due to start in twenty minutes. He gave that quick, alert glance at his watch that she was starting to know. She had the feeling he had a built-in clock and that the expensive Swiss watch served only as confirmation of something he had down to the minute already.

She said it for him. "We'll have to head to the restaurant."

"I've got this image of hot chocolate in my mind," he answered. "Someplace where we could take the boys and not get frowned at when they spill things. But, yeah, there's no time."

"No. Unfortunately."

Pulling up in front of the restaurant fifteen minutes later, he sprang out to open the door for her, while she was still struggling to sit up higher in her seat. He always did that. No fuss or flourish about it. He was just *there,* and so was his hand, ready to take hers and heave. Increasingly, as she got heavier, the heave was good.

Tonight, his breath misted in the cold air and the warmth of his body was like a magnet, drawing her to him.

"Don't come in," she said. "It's two steps to the front door. I'm fine."

"I'll watch." His tone changed as he looked down at her. "I wish we could have had that hot chocolate."

"So do I."

Her breath caught a little. A kiss hung in the air between them like a pattern of snow crystals. Fragile, beautiful, ready to evaporate in a moment. He was watching her mouth, thinking about it, too. His eyes were easy to read, soft and slow-burning. The lean of his body closed the distance between them by another few inches, then her pregnancy bumped against him through her dark coat, a barrier that was as much emotional as physical.

They couldn't do this.

"There'll be someone waiting for you when dinner's over," he said. "Charlie, maybe. Or Alex. You know both of them. They'll let you know when they arrive, then wait somewhere discreet. You'll see me on Monday."

"Thanks."

"Thanks for being so good about the lights."

"No, I'm thanking *you* about the lights."

He smiled, and she did what she had to do— slipped past him as he stepped back, and went into the restaurant.

"You know, I actually am starting to get used to it after all," Lauren told Daniel just over a week later, on Christmas Eve. "I thought I never would."

"People do," he answered, grinning down at her. His dark eyes were warm, and creased at the corners.

Wanting to earn more of that relaxed, cheerful look, she added, "Although I could do without the guy with the missing front teeth."

"That's a bit unfair. He lost them gallantly in the line of duty, you know."

"Well, really it's not the teeth, it's the breath."

"Are you feeding him garlic sandwiches?"

"And the laugh."

"Don't tell him jokes. Seriously..." neither of them was being particularly serious "...he's a good man, but if you like I can rotate him to another assignment."

"No, don't," she answered. "You're right. Charlie's nice. I'm being unfair. And Bill is great, and totally focused."

Lauren gestured through an ice-encrusted window

to where a uniformed bodyguard leaned against his car in the weak December sunlight. His shoulders were hunched and he looked cold, but he didn't take his eyes off the stream of cars entering the parking lot adjacent to Daniel's church.

"Yeah," Daniel agreed. "He's the best."

"Mmm."

Lauren didn't want to admit that, increasingly, the only bodyguard she actively enjoyed having around was Daniel himself. And that was for all the wrong reasons. Like those big grins he'd just given her. The threat to her safety had not escalated any further over the past few weeks, but neither had it disappeared. Just when she was starting to relax, another letter would arrive through the company mailroom, although there had been no more damage to her property.

Nominally, the police were still working on the case, but she suspected that Daniel's security detail was having a negative effect on their enthusiasm. Since she was well-protected, more urgent or serious cases repeatedly bumped this particular investigation back to the bottom of their file tray.

Unfortunately, Daniel's job was simply to protect her, not to investigate where the threat was coming from. She could tell that his mind was quietly engaged on the problem, as he'd asked her several cryptic questions, but like the police, he had other things to deal with.

She couldn't, in all fairness, have asked for more. He already covered this assignment whenever he could, and she was sure that he was skimping on his executive role at Lachlan Security Systems right now, purely for her sake. Or rather, her father's. Inherited from his own father, Daniel's sense of honor and duty was very well developed.

Like her own, his faith was quiet and sincere, as well. This was her fourth visit to his church. Lauren knew Daniel had been surprised when she'd first told him she planned to attend, and even more surprised that she'd continued to come each week. It wasn't just the initial question of security that he'd raised with regard to her own church. She'd found that she liked the warm and welcoming atmosphere of Daniel's church better than the rather stuffy and formal congregation downtown which she'd belonged to for many years.

This morning, she had volunteered for nursery duty, and Daniel had brought his boys. They were already on the floor, playing with trucks along with several other children. The spacious room was bright with Christmas decorations. There was a Nativity scene set up in one corner, and after the morning service, a party was scheduled to take place here, complete with carol singing and a visit from Santa.

Before Daniel went next door to the church itself, she had time to tell him, "The mailroom picked up another letter on Friday, by the way."

"You didn't tell me!"

"I didn't want to ruin your weekend." Keeping him from running his company properly was one thing, but keeping him from his kids was worse.

"Neither did the police, apparently," he answered. "They didn't tell me, either."

"My request. It's okay. I've brought a photocopy."

She handed it to him and he read in a rapid mutter, "'Be warned! Your personal bank account and credit card details have been accessed via the internet. The Van Shuyler Corporation's accounts are next. Cover Deveson's debts voluntarily or watch the decision get taken out of your hands.'" He looked up. "More specific than the other letters."

"Seems like it's an empty threat, though. My accountant ran some checks, along with a police expert, and neither of them could find any evidence that anyone has accessed my personal accounts or the company's."

"If that information was what they got from your file drawer—"

"They could have used it weeks ago," she agreed. "But I don't keep financial information there."

"What *do* you keep there? You told me nothing was missing."

"Most of it's personal. Old diaries and letters and photos. Lecture notes from college that I should probably throw out."

"Our guy was probably pretty disappointed, then."

"Unless he wanted to read the extremely bad poems I wrote when I was fourteen, or find out the names of the boys I had crushes on."

"Yeah." Daniel frowned, and Lauren could see the wheels turning in his mind. Then his tone changed. "Speaking of boys and crushes, let's stop that, guys."

He swooped down to floor level and separated Corey and Jesse, who had started throwing blocks at each other. They were still laughing about it, but their aim was getting harder and better, and one of them would score a direct hit soon.

"You guys have fun," he told them. He was still crouched down at their level, and the fabric of his casual dark gray pants stretched tight across his thighs. "Daddy will be back in a bit, okay?"

"Daddy go church?" Jesse asked.

"That's right, buddy."

"I come, too?"

"Not today. Lauren's going to play with you."

"Lauren read story?"

"Yes." He disengaged himself from two pairs of clinging arms, smiled at Lauren and left the nursery.

Lauren knelt awkwardly on a cushion on the floor and each little boy brought her a book, as did another girl named Emily who was around three years old. All three of them tried to sit on her lap, which was difficult as there wasn't even room for one child there right now. Her baby was due in less than four weeks. Eventually, she managed to get them seated beside her, with the little girl, Emily, perched on a chair just behind.

It felt right. Inside Lauren, the baby was kicking uncomfortably. Daniel's boys only wanted stories about trucks, which didn't please Emily at all. She wanted to hear about Christmas, and said so about sixteen times. No one sat still, and someone had got something sticky all over Lauren's stretch maternity leggings. It wasn't the soft-focus scene of peace and love that it was supposed to be, but it felt right all the same.

Eventually, Emily went to play with another little girl around her own age, and Lauren was left with Corey and Jesse, who decided to treat her like a piece of gym equipment. They were so delightful that she just had to scoop both of them into her arms for a hug and a kiss—she could love these kids so easily!—and that was when Daniel appeared in the doorway, because the church service was over.

For some reason, she felt as if she'd been caught out, and her laugh was self-conscious. "They've given me quite a workout." She still had her arms around Corey and her chin was resting lightly against his curly head.

"You don't have to permit it," Daniel said.

"Oh, but I like it. It's…good for me, or something."

Why was he watching her so intently?

As soon as she framed the question in her mind, he gave a token smile and turned away, stepping aside to let some other parents pass.

"Party time!" said one mother.

Some of the bigger children echoed the words. "Party time! Yeah!"

Daniel's boys immediately jumped up and said, "Yeah!" too, catching the mood of excitement from the other children, although they didn't really understand what it was about.

Lauren wasn't sure what she should do. Bill was still waiting outside to shadow her home. He would watch her place while she packed an overnight bag, and then he'd shadow her to her father's luxurious weekend home near Princeton, where they were spending a quiet Christmas together.

*When is our Christmas ever anything but quiet?*

It was a disloyal, unfair thought, but it hovered persistently in the back of her mind all the same. Eileen Harrap was joining them for Christmas lunch, but then she had her sister to go to in the evening. Lauren's sister, Stephanie, couldn't make it from Europe this year, although she was coming two weeks later for Lauren's baby shower. No other celebrations were planned, no other guests were invited.

Wasn't it a little sad that a kid's church party was the best prospect she had for Christmas color and laughter and life? She wasn't even a parent yet. There was no role for her here.

"I should probably go," she said halfheartedly aloud, to no one in particular.

Daniel heard. He had just come up to her to confirm

her plans for the next few days. But he caught the reluctance in her tone at once.

"Don't you want to?" he asked.

She had a tight, sad look around her eyes. He fought his need to respond to it. Protecting her professionally was one thing, starting to care about how she felt was very different. It scared him and he didn't want it.

Once again, she flushed. "Oh, you know, I was wondering if I should get in some practice at this stuff."

"I think on-the-job training is the only kind that really counts in the parenthood business, but please stay. You're more than welcome."

"I could help."

"That's always good," he agreed.

She nodded and went to ask congregation dynamo Dorothy Minter what she could do. Dorothy pointed her toward the kitchen, where people were bringing out covered dishes of food. Daniel watched her all the way, swinging Corey into his arms and propping his little diaper-padded bottom on hip and forearm. Corey began to play with his ear.

As always, Lauren looked beautiful. Her hair, the color of polished rosewood, was coiled and clipped on the top of her head, and her dark Christmas green leggings-and-top outfit draped softly over her pretty figure. Her legs were still great, and you still wouldn't have known she was pregnant if you only saw her from behind.

Desire stirred inside him like a lion waking from sleep. He'd spent the past three weeks pushing it down, squashing it, stomping on it, the way he'd have squashed a garden bug that was eating his plants. Sometimes he kidded himself that the effort had paid off.

Yes, definitely. He hardly thought about that last kiss anymore. Hardly ever let his fantasies gallop ahead to the point they could have taken it to that night if they'd wanted. She was an assignment and nothing more. He could reel off the names of her most frequent contacts. He could list the restaurants she liked and the stores she shopped at. He knew the outward details of her life, and that was all he cared about.

Wrong! He knew so much more than that, and the more he knew, the more she drew his reluctant curiosity. She was such a mix of qualities. Just when he thought he understood her, she surprised him yet again.

She was courageous and matter-of-fact about the threat to her safety, yet timid and uncertain about her future role as a mom. She was efficient and in control in her professional life, but apparently at sea about her personal future. She could laugh at his teasing humor one minute, and seconds later he'd see tears glistening in her eyes. She was so poised in the way she skimmed through the room with plates of Christmas cookies and finger sandwiches, yet she flushed and stumbled over her words as soon as someone asked her about the baby.

She must have felt him watching her, because her gaze met his across half a room then flinched away again.

Damn it, she scared him, and he didn't know why.

Or maybe he did. Didn't he know that look she'd just given him? Becky used to look at him that same way, years ago, when she was just his office manager and there was nothing personal between them at all.

Oh, mercy, how he'd hated that look! There had always been something so watchful and hungry about it. He hated it when a woman made a man feel like her prey in some primal hunt. The look had disappeared from Becky's face for a while after his father's death, to be replaced by a tenderness he'd responded to. He'd radically revised his assessment of Becky at that time. She'd changed. Or he had. Or maybe he'd only just begun to see the real woman beneath the unsubtle façade that so frequently irritated him.

And so he'd married her and they'd been bad for each other from day one. As soon as she was sure of him, she had begun to criticize him in front of his friends. She had become consumed by strange health fads and expensive personal growth seminars. And of course he was at fault, too. They were classic male faults like not being at home enough and not thinking to appreciate out loud the special little touches she made to meals or decor. He regretted it, but it was too late now. The look had come back to Becky's face. Hungry and watchful, but possessive and hostile, too, as time went by.

*What does Lauren want from me?*

More than she was getting. A woman didn't look at a man like that when she already had what she wanted from him, or when she didn't want anything at all. So what was it? She seemed as determined to reject their chemistry as he was. He was protecting her safety as well as he knew how, to the extent that she herself had agreed to. So what did she want?

*Forget about it,* he decided. *Keep to the boundaries. Remind her that the boundaries are there. That's all you have to do.*

"Corey, can I keep my ear, please?" he told the toddler in his arms. "It's a part of my body, and it doesn't want to come off."

Jesse was pulling at his free hand. "Corations. See corations."

"You want to see the decorations?"

"Come, too."

"Yeah, I'll come, too."

They made a tour of the Nativity scene and the Christmas tree. Then it was time to eat, and he let the boys choose what they wanted. They got cake smeared on their faces from ear to ear. When the party food was cleared away, it was time for carol singing, and then Santa came.

Major disaster. The boys were terrified. Wouldn't go near the guy. Dorothy Minter stepped in and tried to encourage them. She wouldn't believe Daniel when he said it wasn't a big deal, next year would do.

"Oh, but you must get a photo!"

"Let's not make them cry, Mrs. Minter. That'll just scare the other little ones."

"But I'm sure if we just distracted them."

He had to invent an urgent diaper crisis to put her off. When he finally made his escape toward the bathroom, with a kicking child tucked under each arm, he wasn't prepared to find Lauren watching him again.

With that look on her face.

"Maybe you should go," he told her, his cool distance very deliberate, but far more blatant and unsubtle than he'd intended. "Or Bill will be late getting home to his family."

He was rewarded with just what he'd wanted. She recoiled. Her face fell. She began to apologize.

Cutting her off, telling her it was fine and Bill would handle it, he wished her a merry Christmas. Daniel knew he had just condemned himself to spending the entire holiday feeling like a total heel. He hated to hurt her like that, but it was best for both of them in the long run, he was certain. He had nothing to offer her—not friendship, not wisdom, not any kind of involvement—and he wanted to signal the fact loud and clear.

## *Chapter 7*

"Eileen, you have surpassed yourself this year," Lauren's father said, gazing at the wall-mounted singing plastic fish he had just received as a Christmas gift.

"Well, you know you are the world's hardest man to shop for," she answered, unrepentant. "I'm not even going to try anymore. You are getting novelty gifts from me from now on."

Dad laughed comfortably, then said, as if it was a chore, "Well, I suppose we should eat. The caterers have left everything in the kitchen in warming trays, we just have to dish it up."

Sixteen years ago, Christmas hadn't been like this. Lauren's mother had made a big fuss over the holiday season, and if she didn't have enough family available to eat the huge Christmas dinner she'd prepared each year, she invited friends. The following year, she had been gravely ill and she'd died on December 28, when

Lauren was just fifteen years old. The Van Shuyler family Christmases had been *quiet* ever since.

Lauren understood the reasons for it perfectly, which was why she'd never resisted her father's we'd-better-go-through-the-motions attitude. This year, however, a slow-burning fire of rebellion was building inside her and she was determined that next Christmas things would be different.

She would have a child then. A child who would be crawling or even toddling, captivated by colors and lights, constantly putting things in its mouth. She was determined her baby wasn't going to experience Christmas as a tepid, adult-orientated celebration.

Her baby was going to experience Christmas the way Jesse and Corey Lachlan did, with a church party and a drive around the suburbs to look at Christmas lights, a huge, fragrant and brightly decorated tree brushing the ceiling with its topmost branch, a lavish meal, a big gathering of people and a visit from Santa Claus.

Yes, just like Corey and Jesse, only maybe without the yells of terror when the man in the big red suit appeared. Lauren smiled at the memory of their forthright words. "Don't want to see Santa! Don't want to see Santa!"

Then she felt a twist of pain inside her as she relived Daniel's cool suggestion to her just a minute later. She hadn't expected him to push her away like that. She'd thought they were getting on pretty well. They were staying within the boundaries they'd both set. She'd even have said that they were building an unlikely kind of friendship.

But the coldness in his face as he'd spoken to her had looked so deliberate, and she couldn't think of anything she'd said or done to earn it. He was the one who'd first suggested she attend his church. All she'd done was to linger at a kids' Christmas party at which she didn't really belong. She'd watched Daniel's relaxed interaction with his kids, immersed in her usual wistful fear that she wouldn't be nearly as good at the parenthood thing as he was, and as she wanted to be. That was *all*.

At least she didn't have to see him for a couple of days, she thought as she sat down to lunch with Dad and Eileen.

Wrong!

This consolation prize of a fact was shattered just one hour later, after they'd eaten, by the sound of the phone. Her father picked it up, made some terse responses then told Lauren, "That was someone from Metropay Parking." She recognized the name of the pay-parking concession that operated the parking garage next to Van Shuyler corporate headquarters. "Someone has spraypainted graffiti all over the wall of your spot."

"The one where my car was parked when its tires were slashed? I haven't used it since."

"Evidently the guy doesn't know that." Her father picked up the phone again.

"You're going to call the police?"

"No, I'm going to call Daniel. I've had enough of this. The police aren't putting any manpower on it. Daniel can come right over here and we can talk."

"Dad, you can't! It's Christmas!"

"You think he won't have finished his ham?"

She came forward and put her arms around him. "Remember, Dad," she said softly. "Remember the knee-deep piles of wrapping paper, and the little cousins with flushed cheeks and sticky lips? Remember the smells of all the food, not trucked in by a caterer, but things Mom had cooked herself? Remember the trivia games Uncle Pete used to make up to entertain the adults, and the Balloon Olympics he organized in the basement for the kids?"

"Yes. Yes, of course I do." His voice was thick.

"We never made the effort to get together with Mom's family when Uncle Pete moved to Chicago the year after Mom died, but you know what? Somewhere out there, there are people who still do that stuff at Christmas, and I know Daniel is one of them. You *cannot* ask him to come here for a business meeting today!"

For quite some time, Dad didn't reply. Lauren felt his cheek scrape awkwardly against her hair and felt the familiar scent of his shaving cream.

Then at last there came a scratchy, "Point taken. We'll have a child here next Christmas. We'll do it differently. Will you at least let me call him?"

"Will you be able to forget about the whole thing if I don't?"

"No. You know I won't. You're too important to me, Lauren, and I'm sick over this new thing."

"Then call. Make it quick. What did the graffiti say, anyway?"

"The Metropay guy wouldn't repeat it. Apparently, it was pretty obscene." He picked up the phone, keyed in Daniel's number and reported what had happened.

For a minute or two after this he was silent, apart from the odd monosyllable, until Lauren suddenly heard, "Bring the boys as well. No, you're more than welcome. There are some toys I can hunt up from the basement, and it'd be great to get a taste of kids around the place again. Thanks, Daniel, I'll see you in an hour or so."

He met Lauren's glare a moment later without flinching. "It was his idea."

"You could have told him no!"

"I want him here, Lauren. I want his input."

Lauren suppressed a sound of violent disagreement and waited for the inevitable.

"You're right," she agreed an hour and twenty minutes later. "They're obscene."

Daniel had gone to the parking garage on his way through the city and had taken some snapshots of the messages, sprayed in red paint on the wall nearest her space. His boys were building block towers in the great room with Eileen, while the other three adults held what Dad was calling "a crisis meeting."

He had brewed coffee and they were in his study, which was filled not with file cabinets and bound company reports but with books on the North American wildlife and flora that was her father's passion in his spare time.

"And I think you're right, too, John, in feeling we may get further on this if we stop looking to the police," Daniel said. "This is an insignificant case, as far as they're concerned. I want to look at what we know and see what it suggests."

Lauren had known he was working on the issue privately, but she hadn't realized he was already this organized about it. He spread out a printout detailing the dates of each letter, the postmark on each envelope and the wording of their contents, as well as the facts they had on the other incidents. The tires, the file cabinet and now the graffiti.

"If there's a pattern to any of it, it isn't obvious," Daniel said.

"Except that our guy specializes in making my holidays memorable," Lauren commented. "The tire thing was the day after Thanksgiving."

Dad laughed. "Note that down on your profile, Lock. Perp dislikes turkey."

"I might just do that, because otherwise my profile is looking pretty thin," Daniel answered. "Ben's company had approximately sixteen thousand investors, all over the United States. The letters have been mailed from six different locations, according to their postmarks. Two different post offices here in Philadelphia, two in the Boston area, one in New York and one in Connecticut. Three of the letters have useful prints, from three different sets of fingers, but they didn't match anything the police have on file."

He shrugged.

"You don't have any training in this area, do you?" Dad asked.

"No, I don't. You won't be treading on my toes, John, if you hire someone who does. My expertise is in preventing crimes, not solving them."

"I don't want to do that. Not yet." He got up and began to pace the room. "Have you told Ben about any of this, Lauren?" he asked.

"No, we've hardly communicated at all. I'm still waiting to hear what he wants to do about the baby."

"You should. Tell him, I mean. Maybe it'd prod him at least a small step in the right direction."

He shook his head slowly, as if the enormity of Ben Deveson's failings was more than he could handle. Lauren was flooded with the renewed surge of determination that always hit her when Dad seemed out of his depth. She could handle Ben, whatever he came up with. She could handle her mysterious stalker. Ben didn't need to hear about it. She was fine.

"I'm going to sleep off my lunch for an hour." Dad

went on. "Why don't you two take those little boys for a walk? Lauren, you look like you need some fresh air."

Yes, but not in Daniel's company.

She didn't say it out loud, just nodded. Dad looked tired. This whole business was getting to him more than it was getting to her. She shouldn't have pushed him on the Christmas thing.

"I'll get my coat, Daniel."

"I have the boy's snowsuits in the car."

"I'll chase them for you, and you can use the time to think. Dad's right about the fresh air."

"I'm not convinced you could chase anything faster than an inchworm," Daniel told Lauren after her father had left the room.

He was hoping to earn a laugh, but all he got was a half smile. Was she angry or just wary? She had a right to be both, after the way he had frozen her off yesterday. His remorse didn't suggest a useful strategy for getting over the problem. Apologize? Only if he wanted to start what would have to be a very uncomfortable discussion. Kiss her, maybe?

*Oh, yeah, I like that idea,* his body said.

No.

How many times had he already started back at square one with this woman? He didn't want to have to do it again. At some point, surely, their relationship had to *progress!* Ships in a stormy sea eventually reached port. Even after the darkest night, dawn did break. At some point, he had to stop simultaneously wanting her and distrusting her, and hating himself for both feelings. At some point, what he felt toward Lauren had to become safe.

*Solve it, then you can get out of her life. Find the guy.*

Like Lauren, he was intuitively sure that it was a guy. But who?

Out in the big garden, the boys soon had bright pink cheeks. They toddled on legs that were stiffer than usual, thanks to their thickly padded snowsuits, one sky blue and one bright red. There had been a heavy fall of snow in this area about a week ago, and deep drifts of it still remained in hollows and beneath trees.

They loved the stuff, and Lauren responded to their squeals and laughter by getting pink-cheeked and active herself. They made snowballs and a very small, lumpy snowman. Her father had produced an old red plastic sled, into which both boys just fit. At their age, they didn't need a high-speed ride, so Lauren pulled them along the flat, crunchy drifts and they acted as if it was the Space Mountain ride at Disneyworld.

She looked like a big, pink glacé Christmas cherry in her bright cherry-crimson coat with matching hat and gloves. Daniel didn't realize how hard he was grinning at the whole scene until his face started to ache.

How come he couldn't stop watching her? How come she looked away so quickly every time she saw him doing it? Her hair had fallen out of its clip at the back and was bunched up above the collar of her coat. Her nose was getting shiny with cold. She kept pressing those sweet lips of hers together to keep them warm and stop them from getting chapped.

At one point she tripped and almost fell against the snow. He lunged toward her, but she shook her head. "I'm fine. I'm off balance these days."

"You sure? Do you want to go in?"

"I'm fine," she repeated, lifting her chin and throwing him a stubborn grin.

*I want to do this for her,* he realized. *It's nothing to do with being able to get out of her life once the thing is solved. Even if I thought the police would crack this case tomorrow, that wouldn't be good enough. She's had such a rough time—including from me!—yet she's still here, chin up, laughing and waddling around like a tipsy duck.*

*I want to do this for her.*

"Their gloves are sopping wet, Daniel, and their fingers are frozen. They're going to start crying soon."

"He's a kid. He's got to be. It's the only thing that fits."

For a moment, Lauren didn't understand, but then she looked at Daniel's face. His dark eyes glittered and there was an energy and triumph to his expression that was new. Somehow, he looked bigger than usual. His strong shoulders looked even broader. His stance was as solid as the trunk of the oak tree just behind him.

And he was punching one gloved fist into the palm of his other hand as if it was a baseball and he was ready to pitch.

"You mean the guy," she said.

"Yes." He bent down and pulled off Jesse's sodden wool gloves. "Gee, you're right about their fingers. Let's get them inside."

He picked up both boys and they settled into their usual position on his hips. Corey began to whimper, and Daniel asked, "Quick, what can I distract them with?"

"A promise of hot chocolate with marshmallows on top?"

"Did you hear that, guys?"

"I'm sorry, I should have looked at their gloves sooner."

"No permanent damage. I want to think about this some more. About our guy. Out loud."

"I'm interested."

Way too interested, Lauren decided.

Not just in "our guy." In the way Daniel's strong legs moved when he was in a hurry. In the way he narrowed his eyes and stuck his tongue between his teeth as he thought. In the way he managed to deal with his boys and think about the problem of the stalker at the same time. Men weren't supposed to be able to do that with kids the way women did. The six-things-at-once thing. Daniel, she guessed, had had to learn.

"At college, probably," he said. "A *young* college kid. Not as bright as he'd like us to think, because if he's seriously trying to hack into your bank accounts, he hasn't gotten close to doing it."

"Not according to the checks we've been able to make."

"So he's a lightweight. That doesn't mean he's not dangerous."

"Why, though, Daniel? Here, let me take one of the boys."

"I'm fine." They'd almost reached the house. "I'll sit them by the fire and warm them up while you get the hot chocolate."

"Will you have one, too?"

"Yes, please. And as to why, why do I think it's a college kid, do you mean?"

"Yes."

"It was what you said about him making your holidays memorable. His home must be here in Philadelphia, but he's at college someplace else. Boston, probably. His personal appearances in your life are limited to vacation times. This is a game for him, not a full-time occupation. Or that's the theory, anyhow. I could be way off base."

They went in through a side door and she led the way to the great room, where an open fire was burning. Daniel set the boys down in front of it, and they held out their reddened hands.

"They're brave little guys," she said. "I thought they'd really howl."

"Yeah, they're okay kids," he said casually, then grinned.

She saw it and grinned back. "Like they're not the most precious beings you could ever imagine, Daniel Lachlan!"

"All right, don't push the point. They're *extremely* okay. I feel like I've solved this," he said. "I shouldn't."

"Haven't you solved it? I'm totally impressed, so far."

"It's not solved," he insisted, bending down to peel the boys out of their snowsuits.

"Hot chock-it right now?" Jesse asked in a hopeful tone.

"Almost right now, buddy. We just know which track to take," Daniel added.

"That's a lot, isn't it?" Lauren had learned to follow his switches from kid-speak to adult conversation. She was as proud of the new skill as she'd have been if she'd upholstered a couch or re-tarred a driveway. "A lot more than we had to go on a couple of hours ago. I'll put them in the dryer in a minute," she finished, taking the damp suits.

"We have to convince the police to look at it that way."

He still wouldn't take credit and she didn't push it. Instead, they focused on the boys and their wet clothes. It was tough for two-year-olds to drink hot chocolate neatly, she found. The rich, sweet drinks made them sleepy, along with the effects of fresh air and firelight. With Jesse nestled on her lap, slurping hot chocolate and still enchanted by the open fire, she felt a strange new sensation of warmth pooling inside her.

What tender skin and silky hair he had. How focused his big, round eyes were. He hadn't even noticed that she was watching his absorption in the flames. Impulsively she kissed his cheek. It felt like warm satin. Would her own child be this perfect, this bright, this happy? Daniel was lucky. Luckier than he knew.

He didn't seem like he was in a hurry to leave. He stretched himself back on the fat chintz cushions of the two-seater couch, while Lauren sat in the matching armchair. Now that they'd finished their hot chocolate, the boys simply lay down on the rug, and were soon hypnotized into sleep by the dancing blue and orange flames.

"How long will they sleep?" she asked.

"Two hours, if I let them. But then they'll be up until midnight, so I'll give them maybe an hour. Listen, I only let it happen because I wanted a chance for us to talk in peace."

"About the guy? I'm kind of—"

"No, not about the guy."

"I'm sick of the guy," she said.

"I know. I meant I wanted to talk about what I said yesterday. Telling you to go, because you were making Bill late. It was…pretty rude, and I've been wanting to apologize ever since."

She had two choices. Accept it or challenge it. The first choice would be the easiest.

*But I've gotten into the habit of taking the hard road since last spring,* Lauren realized. Seconds later, she heard herself saying, "If that's true, why did you say it in the first place?"

Daniel's choice now. Hard road or easy? She could see him making it, weighing it. After a thick pause, he finally answered, "I don't know." His expression was closed, discouraging any kind of challenge.

She was shocked at the level of her own disappointment. It was like the sharp cut she'd accidentally sliced into a finger a couple of months ago while cooking one of her obsessively nutritional meals. Now as then, understanding kicked in before pain. He was lying, and it hurt.

She hid it well, though. "Let me know when you work it out."

He stared into the fire. "Yeah, I'll do that."

Another fob off, and more choices. Get angry? Let it slide?

Oh, for mercy's sake, it was a little thing, compared to the litany of raw, emotional moments they'd shared.

Maybe he didn't agree.

He shifted on the couch and added, growling the words, "I'll let you know, Lauren, when I've worked out why everything I feel about you scares me so much. For now, 'I don't know' will have to do."

"Okay," she answered lightly, as if it didn't matter.

The problem was, everything about Daniel Lachlan was starting to matter to her more and more, and fighting it just wasn't working.

"It didn't check out." Daniel raised his voice as he spoke into the phone, to drown out the sound of his boys yelling and running up and down the hall.

"I'm sorry?" Lauren asked, at the other end of the line.

"No, *I'm* sorry. It's the boys." He reached behind him with one foot and kicked the kitchen door shut, bringing a slight reduction in the volume of noise. It was just quiet enough for him to hear her laugh.

"Don't ever apologize for those little guys, Daniel," she said. Her voice was warm and a little husky. "They're great, and I love them."

It wasn't just a throwaway line. He knew she really meant it. The idea made him emotional in a way he didn't have time to analyze right now. With difficulty, he returned to the reason for his call. "I wanted to tell you that I just had a call from the police."

"Yes? Tell me!"

"It's not great news, Lauren. They followed through on all Ben's investors in the Philadelphia area—anywhere close to the Philadelphia area, in fact—and my theory didn't check out. There was no one with a kid, male or female, at college in Boston. The closest was a senior at Georgetown University in Washington, D.C. They interviewed him and the facts didn't fit. I'm sorry."

He heard the familiar phrase drop yet again from his mouth and swore under his breath. "Lauren, all I ever seem to be doing at the moment is delivering these apologies to you. I hate it! I really thought I was onto something last week."

"It's not your fault. Maybe it was just a coincidence that the tires and the graffiti both happened around holiday times."

"But it fit. It was more than a coincidence. It felt like it fit."

"I know."

"I'm going to be a little late picking you up, is the

other reason I'm calling. My mother can't get here to mind the boys until seven."

"Cancel if you want," she offered at once.

"I don't want. That part of the assignment I can do. Your dad wants me to take you to the Van Shuyler corporate New Year's party, and I'm going to do it. I'll be so intent on scoping out the terrain, watching your back and surveilling anyone you speak to that you'll have the worst evening of your life. But, hey, at least I'll be there, doing my job. And I'll bring you home in one piece."

She laughed, a warm, delighted gurgle, and he felt a ridiculous degree of satisfaction.

What was it with this woman and his response to her? All the things he couldn't do for her, all the ways he kept failing her and now he was preening just because he could make her laugh? He seriously wasn't holding out a lot of hope for staying awake until midnight tonight. At this rate, the way he assessed his odds of giving her a good time, he'd have delivered her home and he'd be tucked up in bed himself by about ten forty-five.

Wrong. By hook or by crook, Lauren wasn't going to let that happen.

He got the first clue to this fact when he picked her up at seven-fifteen. She looked fabulous in a strappy black dress with a velvet-on-chiffon pattern that showed a cinnamon underdress. The dress clung to all the places where clinging was still possible and draped over the places where it wasn't. Her bared shoulders and back were pale and perfect, and his lips almost sizzled with their need to touch that warm, creamy flesh.

She greeted him with a dazzling smile—too dazzling?—and blue eyes that glowed like Las Vegas neon. Since he'd expected her to mirror his own indigestible mix of largely negative emotions, he raised his eyebrows. "You got a late Christmas gift, or something?"

"I talked myself into a change of attitude," she said, picking up a chic little black evening bag and throwing a black wrap of fine wool around her shoulders. Her voice and her movements were crisp, decisive. "This is the year my baby is going to be born. I'm planning for it to get off to a good start."

"There's not much that you take lying down, is there?"

"I'm stubborn, and I'm a fighter," she agreed, closing the door of her town house. They went down the half-dozen steps to where Daniel's car was parked at the curb.

"But what's that story about the oak tree and the reeds?" she went on. "The reeds bend to the storm and survive, while the oak tree stands stiffly and gets torn up by the roots."

"You're expecting to get torn up by the roots?" he asked.

There was an electronic whooping sound as he released the alarm and the locks on his car. It was a dry, cold night and the rivulets of water in the gutters were frozen. He held the car door open for her, then put his hand beneath her elbow, because it was slippery on the ground. She was wearing her unique scent. Jasmine and orange blossom. He should be immune to it by now, but he wasn't. If anything, its power over his senses was getting stronger.

"I just wish I could learn to go with the flow a little more," she said. "I see other people doing it—like you— and I find myself kind of studying the technique."

She slid into the passenger seat, handling the bulk of

her pregnancy and the flowing fabric of her dress with surprising grace.

"Is that what you were doing on Christmas Eve at the church party?" he asked, seeing an image of her face in his memory, suddenly. A particular frown, a particular hunger in her expression. They'd scared him at the time. But if he'd gotten it wrong…

"I guess," she agreed. "Probably. Only it's crazy, because that's going to work about as well as someone trying to learn to play piano by watching a concert virtuoso. Hey, how did we get to this?"

She fixed him with an accusing stare as he started the car, and he laughed and lifted his hands from the wheel, a weight gone from his mind. She was trying to learn to be a parent from *watching* him? From watching *him?* That wasn't scary. It was…funny, really. What answers did he have? None!

"Not my fault," he said. "I asked one simple question about the way you take what life dishes out."

"It wasn't simple," she argued. "It was personal and perceptive, and the kind of thing that makes an expectant mother start thinking too damn much for New Year's Eve! I'm having a good time tonight, and don't you forget it!"

"Is that part of my professional brief? To give you a good time?"

"Believe it, Mr. Lachlan!"

He spared her a quick glance as he drove, and saw her jutting chin and pink cheeks. "Gee, Ms. Van Shuyler, I wonder if I can handle an assignment this tough!" he said softly.

"If necessary, I'll give you some on-the-job training."

"And just how will you do that?"

"How do you think, Mr. Lachlan?"

"Ah…well, I guess I could come up with a couple of ideas."

So she could flirt, too?

It was another facet of Lauren Van Shuyler that he hadn't seen before. This was hardly surprising. There hadn't been many opportunities for her lighter side to show through. He began to look forward to the evening far too much.

This party was the Van Shuyler Corporation's major social event of the year, with an open bar, a sumptuous buffet and live music for dancing. Lauren's father put in only a token appearance, leaving before nine-thirty, so Lauren was left with the task of working the room. She did it with style and grace—an ability that came partly from practice but mostly from an intuition that couldn't be taught.

Shadowing her closely in the crowded venue, Daniel appreciated the way she so carefully spread her attention, the way she committed new names to memory, and the way she managed to move from one group to another without giving offense. She took very little notice of him, which was fine.

At first it was fine. But what was this feeling building inside him as the evening wore on? He couldn't put a name to it, but it didn't feel good.

Okay, yes, she had to chat to the wife of the head of the accounting section. Sure, she had to make sure that the creative director from the advertising firm that handled the lucrative Van Shuyler account connected with the head of the design team responsible for the overall look of the company's outlets.

But did that really mean that the things she said to him had to be limited to, "Get yourself some supper whenever you want, Daniel," and "You can find a partner and dance if you like. You don't have to shadow me at every step. I'm fine."

It wasn't his job to eat or to dance. It was his job to shadow her.

"Your dad wanted me to make sure you weren't overdoing it." He growled the words like a bear with its head stuck in a tin can. It was around ten-thirty now.

"I'm not overdoing it," she answered.

"You haven't sat down, and you've just picked at a few finger foods."

"I'll eat later, when I've talked to everyone."

"If there's any food left, and if you've still got the energy to pick up a fork. You're nearly eight and a half months pregnant."

"I'm fine." Her tone changed and she moved away. "Phil! How are you? Is Cindy here tonight?"

Daniel shored his shoulders up against a wall and watched her continued progress through the room, wondering if she had even noticed he was no longer by her side. Apparently she did eventually, because she came looking for him about twenty minutes later, and told him, "I'm ready to eat now. Want to join me?"

"Just to make sure you sit down."

"Hey, that's why *I'm* doing it! To make sure that *you* do!"

"Yeah, well…"

His tongue felt thick and he couldn't think of anything else to say. Who was this stranger who had invaded his body? He wasn't usually short of words when he needed them. He didn't usually behave like a professional thug, either, watching a paying client in morose silence the entire evening.

If Lauren minded, she didn't let it show, just worked her way through the healthy supper she'd chosen.

"Don't you get sick of grilled vegetables and salad with no dressing?"

*Way to go, Lock, old buddy! This is how you talked to girls when you were sixteen!*

He was so busy cursing himself that he didn't even hear her reply. He tried again a minute later with something inane about the music, felt the muscles around his temples tighten and finally came up with, "Would you like to dance, or something?"

"I was afraid you'd never ask," she said.

She leaned forward to bestow a flirty smile upon him, accidentally offering a far better view than she realized of the contours below the neckline of her dress. He liked those contours. He'd been wanting to get a better look at them for weeks. Taken totally by surprise, he almost groaned aloud at the instant and unmistakable response from his body.

# Chapter 8

*Why did I say it? Oh, why?*

It wasn't even true.

Until she and Daniel had sat down to supper, Lauren had been well on target toward fulfilling Dad's brief for the evening.

"Have a good time, but make sure you talk to everyone you need to first," he'd told her.

Finally, she couldn't see anyone she hadn't greeted or chatted with, and then she had realized that Daniel was no longer a looming and vigilant presence just a few steps away. It was crazy, but she missed him. He hadn't teased or flirted with her since the car ride, but she liked the strong, silent Daniel just as much. Better, probably, in this context. Everyone else was sharing news, making jokes, asking questions. His alert silence was restful, reassuring. It was the same over supper. She hadn't minded a bit that he said so little.

And then, when both their plates were empty, and still he'd said nothing more than a couple of trivial things that, judging by his dark expression, he obviously felt were an irritating waste of his precious breath, she had been so sure that he would retreat to the edge of the room, once more, to watch her. She hadn't wanted that. Her heart was already sinking in anticipation.

Instead, he'd asked her to dance and she'd jumped at him with the bald truth. Yes, she truly had been afraid he was never going to ask.

She wanted him to ask.

It seemed a miracle that he actually had.

They both moved awkwardly into the middle of the dance floor. She was more than eight months pregnant— she was awkward all the time. But what was his excuse? Likely he hadn't wanted to do this at all. He was just being polite and—

One of Daniel's arms, heavy and warm, laced carefully around her bared shoulders. The other curved at her waist. Too much baby there. He moved it across the fabric of her dress until it rested low in the small of her back. Instinctively, she nestled against his chest, hearing his steady breathing, feeling his solid warmth.

"Lauren—"

"Don't talk. I've talked half the night."

"That's fine." She felt his chin come to rest against her hair.

It was the only place in the world that she wanted to be, and she couldn't believe how quickly midnight came. The band's singer finished a swoony love song and announced, "Count down now, folks. No time for a long speech. And it's ten, nine, eight…"

Lauren lifted her cheek from its pillowed position on Daniel's shirt and blinked.

"I'm not going to kiss you," he said suddenly.

"No."

She looked up at his face, five inches away. His lashes were long and thick, screening the darkness of his eyes as he stared down at her. She didn't know what he was thinking, apart from the fact that he'd decided not to kiss her. Which meant that it didn't make sense that his lips had shaped themselves into the perfect shape for doing just that.

"Four, three, two…"

"I am," he said. "I am going to."

"Yes." Much better idea!

"Happy New Year!"

"I'm sorry," he mumbled. "I *am*…"

"Please! Oh, please!"

His mouth touched hers, parting her lips. It clung for a moment, tasting sweet, feeling like warm berries, then he dragged it away. A sound of protest thrummed in her throat. "I'm going to take you home," he said.

"Don't."

"I'm a security consultant for the corporation." His jaw was tight. "I can't do this with the entire corporate staff watching. I'm going to take you home."

"Where no one will be watching you while you kiss me?" She tightened her arms around him.

"That's not what I meant."

"No. I know. It would be nice if it was."

"I'm not going to make love to you, Lauren. I want to. I've wanted to since I first held your body against mine seven months ago, but there are so many reasons not to."

"I want to hear them."

"You know them."

"Remind me. I can't remember any of them tonight."

"We're in the same place, both of us, and it's the wrong place for this."

"Maybe we've moved. I *want* to move. I'm sick of this place, where I can never relax, where everything is planned and scrutinized and worked for and struggled over. I want to do something easy. I want you to make love to me, Daniel."

"Making love isn't easy."

"It's the easiest thing in the world. You close your eyes, and you touch each other, and it happens. I want that." Deliberately, she cupped her hand against the well-fitting seat of his dinner-suit trousers, brushed her mouth whisper-soft and slow across his and heard him groan.

"You could have it," he muttered. "If that's what you're trying to prove, keep pushing and you'll get it, the whole deal."

"Yes..."

"But, Lauren, I want you to tell me no. Think about it, really think about it, for one minute more, and then tell me no."

"I won't."

"You need a man who's going to stick around, who's going to love you like nothing else, and that man's not me. I don't have it in me to be that man. Not now. Not yet. Not after Becky, and not the way your life is, right now."

He didn't mention Ben's baby, but then he didn't have to. She knew it was what he meant.

"Maybe I won't ever have it in me. If you want the truth, that's probably the biggest reason why I never got in contact with you seven months ago, even when it would have been so easy. How much would you hate yourself, how much would you be hurting your baby's future, if you let me into your bed tonight?"

Lauren still had to let him into her house.

In theory, it shouldn't have been a problem. She'd had him in her town house enough times already, checking locks and windows, playing the tape on her answering machine. It shouldn't have been a big deal.

Somehow, tonight was different. The air in every room was thick with their awareness of each other. He searched each space in silence and she followed him and watched him do it. Watched him brushing aside the curtains, opening closet doors, sweeping every piece of furniture with his gaze.

She couldn't stand it.

"There hasn't been the slightest evidence that this is necessary, Daniel. Not for weeks, since we changed the locks. There's only been the stuff that's centered around company headquarters. The graffiti and the letters. No further escalation of the threat, and nothing at all here at the town house. Even my friends have stopped asking about it."

"I'll check your room."

She followed him, angry at his stubbornness, and they collided just inside the bedroom door, when he turned to ask her a question that never got past his lips.

His lips…

Her eyes closed automatically as soon as his arms shot out to steady her, after her pregnancy had lumbered against his hip. She searched blindly for the touch of his mouth on hers and found it by turning her face upward just as his hands came to rest on her shoulders.

"Hell, why is it so hard to resist this?" he breathed.

"Because it's so good."

"That's not enough."

"I know. Stop *telling* me that! Let me have just a few moments where nothing else is important except what I *want,* what I want *now!*"

She anchored his face between her hands and ravished his mouth. A very female sense of triumph and heat uncoiled itself inside her as she felt his response and understood the extent of what she was doing to him. He needn't try to pretend that any of this was one-sided. They both felt it. It consumed both of them.

His mouth was open, slick, hot and hungry. He spread his fingers and threaded them into her hair, loosening it from its clip until it fell. He dragged his lips from hers and buried his face in the slippery waves. She felt tendrils tickling her cheek, felt his hands stroke it back over her shoulders, then drop to cup and lift her breasts. Her nipples peaked instantly, and she shuddered, rocked her hips like an exotic dancer, would have gotten a whole lot closer if the baby hadn't been in the way.

"Daniel, oh, yes!" Her breathing was shallow and irregular and she throbbed all over.

"Do you want me to take you to bed? Do you, Lauren?" He dragged his mouth from hers and gestured at the queen-size bed that dominated the room. "There it is. It's so close. And whatever you might have heard, let me tell you, it's possible when you're this far along and I'm told it can be *real* good. If you don't want this, tell me that now, before we get even closer."

The bed was covered in an antique wedding ring quilt, which Lauren's mother had rescued from a yard sale years ago. She'd had it professionally restored, but it was fragile and Lauren took great care of it. Just tonight, struggling to put on her panty hose, she'd been so tempted to sit down on it.

In the end she hadn't. She never did.

But someone else hadn't taken the same care.

She froze as she took in the evidence.

"That feels like a no," Daniel said. His arms were still tight around her, and she could sense his arousal, mirroring the thickened pool of sensation in her own body. "I should be happy about that, right?" He wasn't happy. His voice croaked with regret.

"Someone's been in here," she said through tight lips.

She felt his gaze slicing to her face. Was she joking? "How do you know?"

"The quilt on the bed. I never sit on it. It's too fragile now. But someone has. Right there, next to the night table. You can see it's not smooth, and one of the seams has split. Just a half inch. The fabric inside the seam hasn't faded the way the rest has, so it stands out. It wasn't like that when I left the house."

"Lauren, there's no evidence of a break-in."

"I'm sure about this."

"I'm not saying you're wrong. I'm saying it's someone who's gotten access to a key since we changed the locks, who knows the alarm code, and who's taken a lot of care that you didn't sense any disturbance. The quilt is pretty subtle. I wouldn't have picked up on it."

"You're right. It's weird, isn't it? Why does a guy spray my parking place with graffiti and then tiptoe around in here—" She stopped suddenly and grabbed his arm, slid her fingers in a jerking motion up the braided muscles. "I wish I hadn't said that. About tiptoeing. It's too creepy." She shuddered, let him go, clasped her hands against her chest. "How on earth did he get in?"

Daniel's arm wrapped around her shoulder like a metal brace, and the chemistry had disappeared, evaporated by the unnerving sense of an intruder's recent presence. She shuddered again, then reined in her emotions like lacing a Victorian corset.

"Creepy," she repeated. "And worse, it just doesn't make sense!"

"That's because we've been looking at it all wrong," Daniel said. "It's not 'the guy.' Lauren, we're looking at *two* different people." He swore. "But I was wrong about the college kid idea. What makes me think I'm any more on the ball with this? Even so, I'm *sure* we're looking at two different people."

"Is that supposed to make me feel better?" she joked in an edgy way. "That I have two people out for my blood? Or my underwear! Two people stalking me, going through my stuff. Oh, mercy, my stuff!"

A prickle of electricity rippled down her spine and she pushed his arm away. "My drawers? My closets?"

She kept most of her clothes in the adjoining dressing room, but there was an antique tallboy in this room, and she kept her underwear in it, laid on tissue paper lining. One of her few truly wicked indulgences was her underwear. She wore, by turns, Italian silk knit tank top and panty sets with panels of lace, saucy French satin teddies and pretty Swiss cotton bras, depending on her mood.

She didn't even think about showing it to Daniel, about what he might think, just pulled open each drawer in turn and found the subtle evidence of someone else's fingers every time—fingers that had been careful, but not quite careful enough.

She didn't say a word, but he could read her expression with no trouble.

"I guess there are times when you being Martha Stewart's more perfect cousin pays off. I could have birds nesting in my pile of boxer shorts, and I probably wouldn't notice. Whoever it was, they obviously realized they had to be pretty subtle."

"It's worse that way," she answered. Her voice squeaked then cracked, and she couldn't control it. "I'd have rather seen everything flung on the floor, and the drawers still hanging open. Like this, it's personal."

She groped out a hand and closed it around his forearm again, needing the ropy hardness and male strength of it. He gripped her in return, his fingers reaching much further around her. They brushed the fine skin in the crook of her elbow, making her body tingle.

"What do you want to do? We'll change the locks again, of course, and the alarm codes, and you'll have to watch your keys like the English crown jewels. Don't leave your purse lying around, even in your own house. Change Bridget's hours so she only cleans when you're home and don't give her a key at all. Don't have any friends over. I can put men on twenty-four-hour surveillance, inside and outside the house. I can put an intercept on your phone line so we can trace the source of any incoming calls. I can help you move to your dad's, or set up a safe house for you."

"No."

"No to which thing?"

"No to all of it, except the locks and the alarm. I refuse to let this defeat me." She took a deep breath. "There's only one new thing I want you to do."

"Tell me. I'll do it."

"I want you to help my sister, Stephanie, organize my baby shower."

*"What?"*

"She can't do it from Paris, the way I want it now. It's only two weeks away. She's had some great ideas. But I want to make some changes. I don't want it just to be my female friends. I want their husbands and boyfriends as well." As she spoke, she saw the understanding growing in his face. "You can set up a TV in the basement and they can watch a football game, drink beer and play poker, or something. I want to ask Bridget to help with serving food, and I'm going to suggest she bring a couple of her family members as well, to help with serving."

"Are you sure?" His voice sounded husky and strained. "A trap?"

"More like just a chance for you to observe without being too obvious. Yes, I'm sure."

"You know what you're saying?"

"Yes. And it's only what you're thinking yourself. This is someone that knows me. This is someone I think is a friend."

Daniel didn't know who was making the most noise, the men in the basement watching football with the wide-screen TV turned loud, or the women in the living room squealing and laughing over baby shower games.

"Help yourselves to more beer," he told eight broad male backs, cast in silhouette by the bright light of the TV screen. The third quarter had just started, and it was a close game.

A few of the men grunted or said, "Thanks," but most ignored him. The husbands or boyfriends of Lauren's prenatal-class buddies and other friends, they didn't look as if they had any sinister motives in being here today.

Daniel had had Lauren's locks changed on New Year's Day, nearly two weeks ago, and Lauren hadn't let her single set of keys out of her sight since. There was no evidence that anyone had gotten in. There had also been two more letters. The way they were worded still made Daniel think of some angry, spoiled college kid who wasn't nearly as sophisticated as he thought he was, but the police had widened the circle of their inquiries, had interviewed several people and still no one checked out.

He strolled back upstairs, disguising the deliberate silence of his footsteps as simply a lazy gait. In the kitchen, Bridget was deftly arranging platters of hot and cold finger foods, with the help of her twenty-three-year-old daughter, Trish. Both women smiled at him and invited him to sample their offerings. They looked busy and content and above suspicion.

He grabbed a couple of steaming morsels and ducked out of the room again, saying, "Deyyishush!" with his mouth half full, like a starving schoolkid.

Prowling along the hall in the direction of Lauren's bedroom, he heard her voice behind him, coming from the center of the party. As usual, its familiar, musical tone arrowed straight to his gut.

"Oh, Catrina, this is gorgeous! Thank you!"

She was unwrapping the gifts, which Stephanie had piled onto a side table when each guest arrived. Including Lauren, there were fourteen women present.

The baby's nursery was silent, and so was Lauren's study. Her bedroom was empty, and he was about to turn on his heel when he heard a noise coming from the adjoining bathroom. The door was closed and probably locked.

He heard a heavy gush of water and thought, *Yeah, okay, that's what bathrooms are for,* then came back to the lounge room, passing the guest half bath on the way.

Its door was open, showing a vase of fresh pink roses on the marble vanity unit, a spotless guest towel folded on the heated rail and a little basket of shell-shaped soaps beside the gleaming faucet.

So why was someone using Lauren's private bathroom? he wondered.

He stole some more of Bridget's finger foods and leaned in the kitchen doorway, where he could see a good stretch of the lounge room through the double doors that opened from it into the dining room. He'd committed the guest list to memory, and he could see everyone on it except Catrina Callahan, Anna Hazelwood and Corinne Alexander. Two of those women could simply be seated in a corner, out of his range of vision.

He paused a little longer.

Lauren looked fabulous today. Her hair was streaming loose, past her shoulders, and her eyes were bright. She wore bright pink—a frivolous, feminine color that she normally disdained in her role as a company executive. There was a softness about her that caught at his heart. Because she was only thinking about the baby, instead of about all the other things she generally had on her mind?

The dreamy, contented look suited her, and he tried to picture how she'd look when she first held her baby in her arms. He felt a sudden need to witness that moment, and it scared him. Associated images from his own past toppled one after another into his thoughts like dominoes. They reeked of commitment, shackles, unhappiness, pressure and failure.

Oh, no, he didn't want to be on hand to see Lauren's face, after all. He was too gun-shy about everything that went with it.

Back down the hall at a stroll, he was alert for the possibility of one of the men coming up the stairs, but heard a chorused roar of male voices that suggested total absorption in a touchdown. Yeah, he wouldn't have minded seeing the game himself, but Lauren had been skewing a few of his priorities lately, and this was one of them. Her well-being was far more important to him than any football game.

The bathroom was still occupied. No more flushing sounds. Instead, he heard the stealthy click of a cabinet door, the slide of a drawer, the rattle of what sounded like makeup or medication containers.

He waited.

The sounds continued while a couple more minutes passed, then he heard the lock click back. The door opened, and there was Corinne. For the length of a heartbeat, her perfectly groomed face betrayed her, but then she set a bright smile in place and said, "Hi, Daniel" as she moved to step past him.

Standing in the bedroom doorway, all he had to do was lean a little and place a strategic hand against the frame of the door to block her exit. His size and strength did the rest.

"I don't think so," he said.

"Please, Daniel!" She gave a little laugh. "I want to see Lauren unwrapping the gift I gave her."

In silence, he stepped into the room and reached back to close the door behind him. Then he placed his hands on his hips like a nightclub bouncer, knowing he was big enough and strong enough to make the physical threat in the gesture extremely subtle without it losing any of its power. He'd give her a minute or two, and he was pretty sure she'd dig her own grave. If she didn't, he'd dig it for her.

As he'd expected, she saved him the effort.

"This isn't what you think," she blurted, after about twenty seconds of tight silence.

"Tell me what I think," he invited her calmly.

"That I'm stealing from her."

"You don't look like you need to do that."

"Exactly!" She looked relieved. "You're in this sort of area professionally, Daniel." Her voice dropped to a seductive, confiding pitch. "I admit, I'm only an amateur, but it's perfectly valid. I'm simply looking for evidence to support Ben Deveson's bid for sole custody, if he decides to make one. He's been weighing his options on this for months, and he wants more facts."

"What sort of facts?"

"Oh, you know the sort of thing. Evidence of drug use, an unstable personality, multiple sex partners. You'd have to understand that in your business, Daniel. Having you around, and all these extra security precautions, has made it much harder than it was supposed to be. But her lawyers will have people trying to get exactly the same dirt on Ben."

"People who pretend to be close friends of his?"

Hell, he'd never been so angry in his life, and she hadn't even blinked.

"Lauren ditched him," she said. Her lips knitted at the corners. "I knew him first! I introduced them, for heaven's sake! Where does she get the right to assume I'm on her side?"

"Maybe because you pretend to be. And how about the slashed tires and the graffiti and the letters?"

"That's not me doing those things."

*No, I didn't think so, but it was worth the question.*

"I don't know who it was," she went on. "It was convenient, at first, apart from bringing you on the scene, because I know Lauren assumed it was all the same person. But then I felt real bad about it. Poor Lauren! I wouldn't have done something like that to her!"

She fixed him with a pouting expression that said, "Feel my pain, I'm a nice person!" then ruined the unconvincing performance when she added, "She doesn't have anything to worry about with the custody thing. The gal is so squeaky clean you could use her as a tablecloth. Ben'll drop it now, I think, which suits me." She smiled. "I don't want Lauren's kid around when Ben and I move in together."

"Right," Daniel answered through his teeth. "Thanks for filling me in. You can leave now."

He didn't say another word, just bent her arm behind her back, held her wrist, opened the door and marched her out of the room.

"You're hurting me," she claimed on a whimper.

"I'm not." His grip was looser than she deserved. "You'll know it if I start to hurt you."

He was tempted. He was so damned tempted! He wanted to jerk her forearm up parallel with her spine. He wanted to see her bend and twist and beg. This woman had betrayed her so-called friend at a point when Lauren was vulnerable, fighting her hardest, and incredibly in need of true supporters.

"Where are you taking me?"

"I'm taking you to the door," he answered. "You're

going to hell on your own. And if so much as the shadow of your little finger appears in Lauren's life again, I'll have the police slap an arrest warrant on you so fast it'll get fused to your skin."

"On what grounds?" she bleated. "What evidence?"

"We've had hidden cameras in here for over a week."

It wasn't true—he'd have liked to install some, but Lauren wouldn't permit it—but his seething anger gave the words a conviction he was sure she wouldn't challenge. If she did, if she was foolish enough to come back for more, he'd break her entire life into a thousand miserable pieces.

When he'd closed the door behind Corinne, he had to clench his fists to stop them from shaking, and he couldn't move for several minutes. Just had to stand here, head bowed and eyes closed, fighting for control.

His need to protect Lauren was so strong that it terrified him. He was angry at himself for not checking Corinne out more thoroughly. He'd ascertained that she had no shares in Ben's company and no past criminal record and left it at that. He hadn't considered the personal angle. He'd also looked into Ben's business affairs as far as he could, but it wasn't his area, and anyhow the police supposedly had that covered. He wanted to catch the next plane to Switzerland to personally draw Ben Deveson's blood. He wanted to go through every piece of police evidence himself, examine every one of Deveson's company files, turn the whole of Lachlan Security Systems into an investigative task force, until the "convenient" second stalker they were looking for had nowhere left to hide.

Most of all, he wanted to hold Lauren's swollen,

vulnerable form, using the male strength of his body as a promise.

*You're safe. I'm here. I won't let you down.*

*That's exactly what I said to Becky. That I wouldn't let her down. And I made both of us miserable. I don't owe Lauren anything. I don't have to step in and do the honorable thing this time, like I did with Becky. I'm not the father of her baby. I can steer clear of the whole mess and save both of us from all the pain and regret that would follow.*

Restless, still angry and with a sore feeling in his gut that he couldn't explain, Daniel prowled back to the kitchen and stole some more of Bridget's tempting nibbles. He ate without tasting a thing, just listening to the sound of Lauren's voice as she exclaimed in delight over the rest of her gifts.

"You had no right!"

"Good grief, Lauren, what did you want me to do? Pat her on the head and send her back to the party? Hand her over to you so you could chew her out in the middle of a sea of wrapping paper?"

The sea of wrapping paper was gone now. It was six in the evening, dark and cold outside. The place was tidied up and everyone had left. Lauren and Daniel faced each other in the middle of her lounge room, which was filled with pretty new things for the baby. The gifts were incongruous as a backdrop to their anger.

"It was my battle!" she told him. "Corinne betrayed *me,* not you! You had no right to do what you did. You denied me the chance to look her in the eye, hear it from her own mouth and tell her what I thought of her supposed friendship! Instead, you confronted her, threatened her, ejected her from my house without my even *knowing!*"

She shook her head, as if further speech was impossible.

"Do you have any idea what a control freak you are?" He almost yelled it. "I was trying to protect you! That's only ever what I'm trying to do!"

"It's not about control."

"No? Like the baby nursery isn't about control, and the child care books and the perfect diet?"

"Yes, those things are about control," she agreed, lightning fast. "And I *know* that. I can see it, and I laugh about it and I go right on doing it. It *helps* right now! This isn't like that. This is about closure, Daniel. Or *Lock,*" she corrected. Her tone dripped sarcasm the way a piece of honeycomb dripped sweet stuff. "You're starting to make a habit of denying me closure, and if you think you're helping, you're wrong. If I'm a control freak, you have an overdeveloped need to protect. Maybe that isn't a concern for you, but it sure as heck is a major pain for me!"

"I'm protecting you because that's what I'm paid to do. You agreed to it, and the fact is, you need it."

"You go way beyond what you're paid for, Daniel!" Her eyes sparked and her voice shook. No one wearing a bright pink tunic and leggings should be able to look that sure of herself. "But when I let you do it, like the times I've taken your tips on how to be a parent and got involved in your church, you've turned on me and lashed out as if I'm trying to smother you or something. You're the one sending the mixed messages."

*My, but you're beautiful when you're angry!*

Yeah, just imagine what she'd do if he really said it! Daniel thought.

His mouth tasted sour. He'd had a beer while he hung out downstairs, watching the game and waiting for the party to end. Then he'd had a second one. He regretted both of them now. They sat in his gut, weighing him down, and blurred the sharp focus that was so important to him when he wanted to think.

He really wanted to think right now, and in all honesty, it wasn't the beer that was preventing it. It was Lauren. She was so electric and magnetic and *beautiful* when she was angry.

"Here's another mixed message for you, then," he told her, and moved forward to kiss her with more certainty and intent and confidence than he'd ever felt about a woman before.

Had he ever kissed a woman this angry before? Most of his experience—Becky, of course, and a couple of others before her—had involved women kissing him, after what he'd only later realized was detailed planning and strategy on their part. He didn't like that crafty premeditation, that sense of an agenda. This was so different, and so much better.

Her eyes were bright and there were spots of hot color in her cheeks. Her loose hair was wild around her face because she'd been running her hands through it and tossing it back as she lifted that fine-boned yet oh-so-stubborn chin. She watched him coming at her, had to know what he intended and just went on glaring at him as if to say, "I dare you!"

He rose to the challenge without a second's pause.

"If you think this is going to make a difference," she said, hissing like a cat. The sharp turn of her head brought his lips to the corner of her mouth, and he tasted the sweetness of strawberries, spongecake and cream.

He cupped his palm to capture her jaw and coaxed

her head back in his direction. Her faltering, "No!" made her lips into a pout, and he branded them with his mouth.

"Say that as if you mean it and I might stop." His voice snarled in his throat.

"I do mean it. It's not going to make a difference. I'm still angry."

"But you're kissing me back."

Oh, yes! He felt her fingers come to rest lightly on his hips. Her face had lifted to meet his now, instead of trying to turn away. Her lips had parted. She was very definitely kissing him back.

"I'm kissing you back," she agreed. She wrapped her arms around his neck, nipped his lower lip with her teeth then salved the nonexistent wound with her tongue. They both had to lean to get beyond the baby. "But it makes no difference. I'm angry."

"What are you going to do about it?"

"Kiss you until you apologize."

"That's a pretty wild claim. I can hold out longer than you."

"Good! I'm in no hurry."

Neither of them were making much sense.

"Then what?" he demanded.

"Then I'm going to call Corinne and arrange to meet."

"No!"

"You're not going to preempt me on this, Daniel. You're not going to stop me from doing what I need to do. Kiss me as much as you want."

"Yes. Yes, I'll do that," he muttered.

"But don't kid yourself that it changes anything about how we deal with each other."

A cold shower wouldn't have worked nearly as fast as Lauren's last speech. Daniel stepped back.

"Don't call Corinne!" he said. "For mercy's sake, don't do it!"

"Why not?"

"Because you have a baby due in eight days."

"So I'm a child who isn't safe fighting her own battles? Stop doing this to me, Daniel!"

"You have *other stuff,* Lauren! That's what I'm saying. Don't give her the satisfaction of finding out exactly how much she got to you. Do you want a catfight with her, like on daytime TV?"

"You think that's my style?"

"No! Heck, no! But maybe it's hers. You're so much better than she is, I can't stand the thought of you even breathing the same air."

She looked at him, head tilted slightly to one side, calmer now than she had any right to be. "I wonder if that's the nicest thing you've ever said to me." A smile tickled the corners of her mouth and brightened her eyes. "I think it is."

"Did you remember you're booked for a tour of the maternity unit at the hospital tomorrow afternoon?" Daniel said, fighting the strange wobbly sensation in his gut. "And that your dad wanted me there to check out their security?"

"Yes, I remembered that. I have a prenatal appointment just before it, and I want you there, too. In the waiting room," she added pointedly. "I *want* your protection, Daniel. But I don't need you to protect me from betraying friends."

He shrugged, hiding his panic. Damn it, she *did* need that!

Or, he suddenly wondered, his stomach caving in even more, was Lauren right? Did the need come purely from him?

## Chapter 9

"How'd it go?" Daniel had been prowling the obstetrician's waiting room, ill at ease with his role.

"Dr. Feldman says everything's fine," Lauren answered. She was back to business wear today, a navy dress that he recognized. "The heartbeat is strong and the baby's still growing. The head is down and well-engaged. That means—"

"I know what it means."

"Right. So you know what it means when he says I've started to dilate, as well?"

"It means you could still be around three weeks from now."

"Ready to commit murder, probably."

"Speaking of which, I didn't ask you yet about whether you—"

She anticipated his question. "Yes, I saw Corinne

this afternoon. Yes, she's still in one piece and has all her hair."

"That's a plus," he agreed cautiously.

"I didn't lose it, Daniel." She brushed her fingers up his gray shirtsleeve, as if soothing a child. Could she tell that something was eating at him? He was tempted to ask her for help in working out what it was. "I sat behind my big desk in my big office with my lawyer in the room. I stayed in control, I forced her to look me in the eye—she wasn't very good at it!—and I got what I wanted."

"What was that, exactly? You never told me yesterday."

"You weren't showing much sign that you'd listen. I wanted to find out more than she intended to tell me about where Ben's thinking is and I achieved that." Her chin lifted, chasing away the delicate shadowing on her neck. "I know where I stand with this baby. Ben's not going to return to the U.S. or he'll have to face charges. He says I can visit him in Europe if I want him to see the baby. 'No hard feelings,' or something. Corinne is planning to join him soon. I never realized that her trip to Europe before Christmas was mainly about cementing their relationship. Well, since she lied to me about the trip, that's hardly surprising! And he's 'sorry' I've been hassled with threats. He's planning to offer some kind of settlement, but I'm not going to accept it. Not when it's really other people's money. I'm not going to take the baby to Europe. I'm on my own."

It felt like a bucket of hot water cascading down his body. He was more emotional about this than she was. But then, she hadn't really been through it yet. Her baby was still unborn. She didn't know what she was getting herself into. Was that why this was unsettling him so bad?

"How does that feel?" he asked, and his voice was husky. "Is it okay?"

"It feels good. Under the circumstances, considering the other options, it feels good."

She gave a wince which suggested it didn't feel good at all, and rubbed her lower back. Daniel knew the gesture. He almost said, "Let me rub it for you," but he was wary today, rethinking a lot of things.

If he'd had his way, she wouldn't have seen Corinne this morning, but it had worked out the way she wanted. She'd said yesterday that it was about closure. Was it a sense of closure that made her look different today?

Calm, a little introspective, happy.

Yes, she looked happy, and it seemed to come from deep inside her. It wasn't like the stubborn and deliberate I'm-going-to-enjoy-this-if-it-kills-me aura she'd worn two weeks ago on the night of the corporate New Year's party. It wasn't even like yesterday's fuzzy glow of pleasure over the baby's gifts.

"What's changed, Lauren?" he asked suddenly, as they crossed a high, glassed-in corridor to the main hospital, from the building where her obstetrician had his office.

She stopped and looked at him. "Does it show?"

"Yes, it shows. It looks great. *You* look great. You don't look so…driven, or something."

"Hormones?"

"More than that."

"Well, then—you're right, I do feel different—it has to be because I know where I am, now, and who my friends are. Not Ben. Not Corinne. Eileen, Bridget, Stephanie, Catrina and the others. They're my friends.

And you." She repeated the word a few seconds later, and this time it was a question. "You?"

"Yes, of course I'm your friend," he growled.

*I'd never betray you,* he almost added, but then he held the words back. Was her definition of betrayal the same as his?

"There's still the guy," he said instead.

"The guy has never bothered me, Daniel. The violation of having someone go through my things bothered me. That was always what got to me, far more than the tires or the letters."

They were standing beside a set of windows that ran the length of this connecting walkway, and much of Philadelphia's downtown business district was visible in the distance.

"Look," she said, pointing. "You can actually see the top of the building where Ben's company had its office space. I noticed it a few weeks ago. The sign is still in place. They had six floors of the building, and I don't think it's been rented out again. Someone must be hurting over that."

"I guess so, yes," he agreed, not really thinking about it.

Or not at first, anyway.

"The tour of the unit is due to start in a few minutes," she reminded him. "We'd better get to where we're supposed to be."

They walked on, in the direction of the bank of elevators.

"They're going to think I'm the father."

"I know. We can put them straight if you like."

"It's not important. Let them think what they want."

Lauren nodded. "If that's okay with you. Who needs questions, or strange looks?"

She was beginning to wish she hadn't arranged her day quite so efficiently, with the prenatal appointment and the maternity unit tour back-to-back, at five-fifteen and five-thirty. She would have liked to sit down. Dr. Feldman's internal exam had been uncomfortable—he said the baby was facing frontways—and she still had a dull, heavy ache low in her abdomen, and a feeling of pressure between her thighs.

It was good to have Daniel here. Why pretend to herself? It was *good*.

She had gotten too accustomed to him, that was the problem. Accustomed to the way he opened doors for her, asked her if she was warm enough or if she was thirsty. Accustomed to the way his frequent watchful silences created a sense of safety all around her. Accustomed to the way he'd break one of those silences with an anecdote about his boys, told in such a way that she always laughed, always accused him of exaggerating and never really believed him when he said he wasn't.

Ouch.

The ache low in her belly suddenly coalesced into actual pain, different in quality to anything she'd ever felt before. Since when did she have a freight train inside her, pushing a twenty-ton coal truck into her back, no warning at all? She sweated it out and it ebbed in about thirty seconds.

It wasn't labor.

Couldn't be labor.

This baby hadn't checked its appointment diary. Labor and delivery were down, in black and white, for *next* week. She was fine.

Fine, and now she was completely unable to focus

on the tour. Daniel's fixed, polite expression of interest looked more genuine, although she knew it wasn't. He was preoccupied with something else, as well.

"You okay?" he asked a little while later, as the group of expectant mothers and nervous dads trooped along the corridor to look at one of the operating rooms available for cesarean deliveries.

"I'm fine," she chirped. "I'm glad they don't move patients to a different room for delivery when everything is going as it should."

"Yeah, it's a nice hospital. Uh, I'm going to make a phone call, okay?"

"Sure."

"Can't use my cell phone inside a hospital, so I'll catch up to the tour. Don't worry."

"I'm fine," she repeated. Seconds later, as she peered into the silent, high-tech space of Obstetric O.R.1, the freight train shunted into her back again.

It wasn't labor. Couldn't be labor. But it sure didn't feel good. A clock high on the wall of the O.R. gave her a piece of information she really wasn't at all interested in. It was a quarter till six. Fifteen minutes since the first pain.

Daniel came back from making his phone call, and his eyes were narrowed so far that they looked like slits.

"Is there a problem?" she asked.

"Not so far. The opposite. I'll keep you posted."

She would have asked him what he meant, only they'd just reached the nursery.

"Wow! Babies!" he said, and he grinned as he looked through the glass. "Haven't seen them as small as this for a while."

Most of them were asleep, but a couple were crying.

One tiny red thing with a shock of black hair was having its first bath, and was not happy about it. The other couples on the tour were holding hands and exchanging private smiles.

Lauren started to turn in Daniel's direction with a smile for him, then remembered why he was here. She made herself say instead, "How is this unit from your angle, Daniel? Is it safe?"

"Yeah, it's good," he answered. "No real problems."

He went through some details on security arrangements, but Lauren wasn't listening. That freight train was attempting another shunting maneuver in her belly. Longer this time. Felt that way. Maybe only because it hurt more. The nursery clock showed seven minutes to six.

Daniel had caught sight of something in her face.

Sheer terror, possibly.

He said something to her, and she didn't hear a word of it, just clutched blindly at his arm. Decided that his arm wasn't going anywhere without her ever again. Couldn't think about the rest of him, right now, but the arm, definitely, was staying in her life.

She must have answered his question without even realizing it, because the next thing she knew, he was... not yelling at her, but it felt that way.

"You're *not* fine! What's wrong? You're cutting off the circulation in my arm. You looked like you were—"

"It's not labor." One of the other couples looked at her and she lowered her voice, to repeat, "It's not labor."

"No?"

"It just hurts. Then it goes. Then it comes again."

"And that's not labor?"

"No. It's those Braxton Hicks contractions. The books

say they can get quite painful." She got a curious look from the nurse conducting the tour and gave a big, reassuring smile in reply.

Four minutes later, the next contraction began, and they pretty much stuck to the four-minute pattern after that. Three minutes till six. One minute after. Five after. Nine after. The tour finished.

"Are you ready to go home?" Daniel asked.

He seemed to accept that she had taken total possession of his arm, which was a plus. It was the best arm in the world. About every four minutes, she knew she'd die without it.

"No, I'm not," she told him. Was it supposed to get this intense, this soon? Wasn't it supposed to build gradually?

"Yeah, I was starting to wonder. It actually is labor, right?"

"I think so."

"And you want to check in for the night?"

"Yes."

*And I don't want you to leave.*

But she didn't have to say it because he didn't even ask. He just told her, "Let's get you settled, and then I need to call my mom, okay?"

"Okay."

"I'm staying, Lauren. I'm not leaving you."

"I know. Thank you." She held tightly to his warm arm the way she'd held her teddy bear after a nightmare when she was six.

They walked the corridor of the unit until Lauren knew every detail of the route by heart. She sucked on ice chips. She leaned her forehead against the wall of the room assigned to her while Daniel pressed his fists into her lower back.

With every contraction, she considered an epidural. But the nurse warned her that it could slow things down, especially with a first baby, and it looked as if things were going pretty slow already. Better to wait until later, when the pain got real bad. With at least five freight trains shunting around inside her now, Lauren wondered what "real bad" could possibly feel like.

Daniel tried to distract her with a running commentary on the wrestling show on the TV in her room, but she was beyond that now. The hands on the clock crawled around some more but meant nothing. The contractions had stabilized at around three minutes apart, but she wasn't dilating fast.

"You've still got a long way to go," the nurse told her.

"I think I will have that epidural now," she decided aloud.

"Okay, honey, but the anesthesiologist is in the middle of a C-section with another one coming up, so he's going to be a while."

She left the room, and Lauren told Daniel calmly, "I hate her."

"Let's go for another walk."

"No!"

For some reason, the crawling clock now claimed it was seven in the morning. Daniel's mother must have stayed all night with his boys. Lauren tried to mind about that, but couldn't. She didn't actually believe that the rest of the world existed anymore. A new shift of nurses came on. From somewhere, she smelled breakfast. Her new nurse told her that the anesthesiologist would be here soon, after one small, tiny, teeny, little emergency that had just cropped up. Lauren didn't believe her for a second. The anesthesiologist didn't exist.

Daniel persuaded her to go for walk number nine around the corridors. She agreed, but hated him.

"Doesn't this help?"

"No! It hurts! I went to the classes. I'm breathing. It wasn't supposed to hurt this bad."

Sobs came, dry ones without tears. They shook her whole body. She clung to Daniel and he held her. Kissed her. Told her, "It's okay. I love you, Lauren. It's okay."

She didn't believe him. Didn't believe the nurses, so why should she believe him? The world was ending, only no one had told her. She wanted the world to end, because then this wouldn't hurt anymore. She wanted to get back to her room, except that the contractions were coming so fast she could only take a few steps between each one, and walking during their iron grip was impossible.

When she at last crawled back onto her bed, Daniel excused himself and left the room. Bathroom. She hated him for needing the bathroom. He was away for three contractions, and they seemed to hurt far worse than any of the others. How was that possible?

"It's okay," he said when he got back.

"It's not okay. I want you here. All the time. I'm not going to be a well-behaved patient. It feels better when I behave badly. I'm not happy, and I *hate* you!"

"It's okay."

"I said I hate you."

"And I love you, okay? I'm here for you. Forever, if you'll let me."

"Go away! No. No, don't go away. Hold on to me. Oh, dear Lord, when will this be over?"

The nurse had once again strapped her onto the

monitor, where the printout of the contractions showed like impossibly jagged mountain ranges, climbing to the very top of the graph. "Pretty intense," she murmured. "The baby's still facing frontways, that often makes it extra bad. Your waters haven't broken yet, have they, honey?" she added.

"No."

"Let me do that for you, and it should speed up this last bit."

Soon. It would be soon now.

The freight trains got serious about doing their job, and the pace and length of the contractions intensified even further. There was hardly enough break between them now for her to take a single breath, and the pain didn't stop. The anesthesiologist was apparently on his way.

Too late.

"A good nine centimeters dilation, now, Lauren, you're doing great!" said the nurse. "The head's way down. It won't be long. You're almost there."

"My epidural…"

"You don't have time now, honey."

"I hate her," Lauren gasped, after the nurse had left the room.

"You mentioned that before," Daniel said. "Except that it was a different nurse."

She grabbed his arms again—both of them now—and gasped and panted, and squeezed those warm, familiar muscles until she couldn't squeeze any harder.

"I want to be rescued," she said. "Remember that night we first met? Didn't it feel great when we got rescued?"

"You have a little more work to do on your own first, this time, sweetheart." His voice was a croak.

"Help me!"

"I'm here, honey. I will. I love you, Lauren."

How many times over the past few terrible hours had he said it to her? Daniel wondered.

Momentarily released from her grip, he pressed his fingers into his eyes to stop the flickering pattern of light that his fatigue had produced. His back and his head ached. Every joint felt stiff. Like the day he and Lauren had first met, in a concrete duct cavity under a broken building, they had people around them and yet they were totally alone. Just him and her, a baby on its way, and a level of inescapable honesty that was more confronting than anything they'd faced physically.

Well, no, he revised. For Lauren, this time it was different. She'd entered a zone of pain that was beyond his own experience. She was walled up inside it, consumed by it, and what she said wasn't honest anymore, it was wild and desperate and beyond logic.

Or so he'd hoped, because she'd said more than once, now, that she hated him.

*While I'm telling her that I love her as if there's no tomorrow.*

Had he actually stopped to think about whether it was true?

The whole world had shrunk out of sight. The only thing left was her pain, her face, her need, her courage and her falling apart. He felt as if he'd do anything to make it go away, to share its inexorable weight. So he'd told her, over and over, that he was here, that he'd never leave.

And that he loved her.

Was this the most heartless piece of dishonesty ever to fall from his mouth, or did he mean it?

*I never said it to Becky,* he remembered, when she was giving birth.

He'd put a lock on his tongue during her labor, so that he wouldn't let fly with something that had never been true. He'd never loved Becky, and he'd refused to demean both of them by saying it while she labored to produce their twins. He couldn't have said it if he'd tried. That was the moment when he'd finally accepted just how bad their marriage really was.

*So am I lying to Lauren now?*

No.

*No!*

These were the best, truest and most liberating words he'd ever spoken. They made him giddy with happiness and hope and relief. Exultant...drunk, almost...with confidence and power. He loved her. He loved everything about her. He already loved the baby that was about to be born, though it wasn't his. The baby was part of Lauren, and that was more than enough.

Her grip on his arm tightened once more and he steeled himself for the sting of her nails digging into his flesh and the painful squeeze on his muscles. He slid his hand along the inner skin of her arm, leaned forward and brushed the damp hair back from her forehead.

She was so beautiful! Even with her face drained and contorted, her hair hanging limp to her shoulders, sweat shiny on her upper lip, her temples, her throat, she was just so beautiful to his sight.

She began to shake, and he said once more, urgently, as if he might never have another chance, "I love you, Lauren!"

She hadn't even heard. "Help me! I have to push! It's coming!"

Yes, but slowly. Too slowly. She gave it nearly an

hour of intense effort, with almost no rest between each contraction, and at last the head crowned. Daniel saw on the monitor the way the baby's heart rate had started to dip dramatically with each contraction, and felt sick with fear. Dr. Feldman had arrived at some point. He hardly remembered when. Now, a second nurse wheeled out the regular newborn warming bed and wheeled in a different one, which even Daniel's untrained eye could see was equipped with specialized features for intensive care.

Lauren was working too hard and was in too much pain to understand that anything was wrong. One final, mighty push and she delivered the head, and Daniel thought it was all over. His little twins had both slipped free with ease at this point. He'd kissed Becky on the forehead.

But this time, it wasn't happening.

"What is it?" he asked the doctor hoarsely. Didn't dare to be more specific in case Lauren guessed there was a problem.

"We're fine. The shoulder's a little stuck, that's all."

All?

Daniel looked at the monitor and saw that the heart rate was way, way down. He knew there wasn't much time. "Get it free!" he hissed between his teeth.

"We're working on that. Pant through this contraction, Lauren," the doctor told her.

She said, "I can't!" on an agonized gasp, then did it anyway. "Huh...huh...huh..." Her eyes were open and staring, fixed, on a point in space.

Daniel felt his own helplessness like a rope tightening around his neck. He would have torn his whole arm off, just to make this a tiny bit easier for her. *You wanted my arm, Lauren. Here, have it, if it helps.* On the clock, each tick of the second hand seemed to teeter and hold its breath before it moved.

"Okay, push now, Lauren. *Huge* push!" Dr. Feldman said.

Daniel didn't want to think about how the obstetrician's hand was positioned.

"Huge, huge push. That's great."

The baby shot out like a cork, almost projecting off the end of the bed. Lauren moaned and began to work her lungs like an athlete after a marathon. She was shaking uncontrollably.

"It's a girl!" the doctor said. There was a silence, then the sound of a strong cry. "There! A beautiful baby girl!"

"Is she okay?" Daniel asked, his voice rasping painfully.

"She's fine. She's beautiful. We're just going to give her a little oxygen… Does she have a name?"

"Callie Jean, after my mother," Lauren gasped, then began to cry. "Oh! Oh! I have a baby girl! I have a precious baby girl!"

"Callie," the nurse said. "That's pretty."

"Mom's name was really Caroline, but no one ever called her that," Lauren said through her tears. "I've always loved the nickname just for itself."

"Here she is, and she's beautiful."

The nurse laid the baby on Lauren's stomach, still slick and red and naked. She was big, with a wet cap of black hair, and she was still crying. Lauren looked at her, her hair shading her face. She said, "Oh!" over and over again, and Daniel thought that he'd never heard such happiness in a human voice, such musical emotion. He could actually hear the smile.

But he couldn't share it. She hadn't asked him to. It made his own love for the baby meaningless, when he'd felt so exultant about the new emotion just a short while ago.

*She hasn't even looked at me,* he realized. His breath tightened and stopped in his lungs. He could hardly see her face. *She hasn't touched me since she stopped needing my arm. "I have a baby girl,"* she said. *She hadn't ever told me she'd decided on the baby's name. In all those conversations we had, she never even mentioned it. This isn't my baby. Lauren hasn't asked me to love her, or to love Callie. What on earth am I doing here?*

"I need to get out of here," he muttered, speaking to no one, hardly able to breathe.

He got himself out of the room as fast as he could. Didn't know where he was headed at first. He was simply escaping. He prowled for several minutes, breathing shallow, limbs shaky, eyes stinging with fatigue. He hadn't eaten for, what, around twenty hours? His stomach was totally hollow, yet he didn't feel hungry at all.

Finally, with a sense of defeat, his mind crystallized and was ready for action. Only one thing to do. The thing he should have been doing all along. The *only* thing he should have been doing.

His job.

Lauren didn't know when Daniel had left. It seemed as if one minute she was squeezing his arm, ready to die, and the next, as she looked up to smile at him, starry-eyed and pain-free, from the magic sight of her baby at her breast, he wasn't even in the room.

"Where did Daniel go?" she asked the nurse.

"He said something about…uh…getting out of here," the nurse said. She looked a little taken aback.

But then, she didn't know that Daniel wasn't this baby's father. He was probably calling his office, or his mother and the boys. He was calling his real life.

"I'm done," he would say on a heavy sigh. "It's been a nightmare of a night, but I'm free now, and I'll be with you as soon as I can."

Something like that.

Lauren had kept him hostage here for about seventeen hours, since the end of yesterday's tour.

*He told me he loved me. I can't remember when, but I know I didn't imagine it. He said it more than once.*

Yes, and what had she told him, almost as often?

That she hated him. It wasn't true. She couldn't think, now, why it had seemed so important to lash out at everyone within reach. But it had felt totally necessary to say it at the time.

If she hadn't meant it, she had to assume that he hadn't meant it, either.

Pain-free, exhausted, euphoric about her baby…then flat.

Flat. Empty. She hadn't known that feelings could ebb and flow like this. Her emotions were like king tides, sweeping in and out, churning everything in their wake.

When she was settled in her room half an hour later, with baby Callie fast asleep in a Plexiglas crib right beside her bed, Daniel still hadn't returned. Maybe he wasn't coming back at all. She was watching Callie when he appeared in the doorway at last.

"Listen, I have some good news." No greeting, no smile, just that.

"Yes?" Her heart was pounding. Just the sight of him,

tall and strong, wearing the long night's fatigue like battle dress, was enough to make her dizzy with need.

And love.

When had it happened? She couldn't pinpoint the moment, or the day, or even the week. She just knew, the way she knew her own name, the way she knew she'd die for Callie, that Daniel was a part of her heart and her soul.

He came toward the bed, then stopped awkwardly, several feet from it. His body was partially masked by Callie's crib.

"I wanted to tell you right away," he said. "I've found the guy. It was what you said about Ben's six floors of office space standing empty that gave me the idea. Ben's shareholders weren't the only ones hurting when he fled the country. He had other creditors, too, and with a company like his, whoever leased him office space would have been high on the list. I had the police check it out last night, and they confirmed it just now. It was a Boston college kid whose father owned the building Ben's company worked out of. They've already made the arrest."

Lauren looked at him across the heavenly vista of her sleeping baby girl. His face looked blank, professional, tight-lipped. She spent about seven seconds debating the issue of whether she should tell him how she was feeling right now.

The answer was yes. Give it to him with both barrels.

"Is that what you think I care about?" she demanded, her voice rising higher and louder with each word. "I look down for my very first peek at my new baby girl, and when I look up again, you've disappeared. I have no idea if you're ever coming back, and when you do, all you can tell me is that they've made an arrest? That's great! It's peachy! You've done your job, and you should be proud. Now you can get out of my life!"

She burst into tears. Pain and release, inseparably mixed. Hormones? So be it! Hormones made a lot of sense. Much more sense than security consultants who were too strong and too competent for their own good.

Daniel came closer. He sat on the bed. He stroked a single finger along the back of her hand. "I love you."

"And I hate you. We had this whole conversation during labor, remember?" She sniffed, snatched her hand away from his delicious touch, mashed a tissue into her face, sniffed again and looked at him. "Do we have to repeat it?"

"You don't hate me," he said.

"And you don't love me. Apparently men and women lie to each other during labor. The truth comes out when the baby's born."

"I *do* love you. I don't know how it happened, but I've let go of something since I met you. A kind of mistrust that was dormant inside me even before my marriage to Becky. It would probably have disappeared in a good marriage, without me even knowing. Becky and I didn't have a good marriage, Lauren."

"You told me that the first night we met."

"And I spent the next six months wishing I hadn't. Denying myself the chance to see you again because I wished so much that I hadn't told you what I did. Scared about the power of the connection we made under that rubble. I love you. And it *hurt,* Lauren, when you didn't include me after the birth. It seemed to me like I didn't count for you then, when I'd just realized that you meant everything in the world to me, and I'd spent the whole night proving it."

"If you knew that, that I meant so much, why did you leave?"

"I left because it hurt too much to stay, feeling like I didn't belong. That you didn't want me, and you didn't even consider that Callie meant something to me, too."

She tried to say that wasn't true, but he ignored her.

"Seemed like the only thing I could do was to do my job. So I did it. I made the final connection that got our guy out of the picture, and now—I love you. If you don't want anything to do with that, fine, I guess I'll just have to learn to live with it, but it's still true, so don't accuse me of letting you down." His words were angry, rushed, intense. "I was there. For you and for Callie. It didn't look like you wanted me. If you do want me, tell me that, don't yell at me about leaving you. I'm here, I want to marry you, and if you say yes, I'll be here for the rest of your life."

What could a hormonal postpartum new mother do, after a speech like that, except burst into tears?

"Why am I doing this?" she whispered, her voice jerking in her throat. "The sun has just come out in my heart, and instead I'm sobbing like it's broken."

"Gee, yeah, so strange," Daniel whispered, kissing the tears away. "Couldn't be seventeen hours of horrible pain and no food or sleep, could it?"

"You know, the pain really wasn't so bad."

His shout of laughter could have been heard six floors away, and his grin could have lit up three counties. "Tell that to my arm!" he said. "I'm still wondering when the feeling's going to come back in it."

"Poor arm." She held it again, softly this time. Used

it shamelessly as leverage to pull him closer once more. "And it's still wearing a business shirt, too. I'm glad you took off your tie."

She stroked his jaw and his warm neck, reached her hand behind his head and made it quite clear to him exactly where she wanted his mouth. He obviously had the same idea. Time seemed to stand still as their lips met. He didn't let her go until they heard a strange new sound behind them.

Callie. Crying.

A nurse came in and said cheerfully, "I think she's hungry, Mommy. Are you planning to breast-feed?"

"I'm hoping to," Lauren answered, a little nervous. "Are you, um, giving lessons?"

"That's why I'm here, and I know you'll do fine." She turned to Daniel. "Would Daddy like to hold his baby girl, while Mom and I get ready?" His baby girl. The words sounded so right—as right as the way Daniel's little boys felt in Lauren's arms when she hugged them. She knew now that he felt the same. Would he say it? If he said it, her happiness would be complete. In silence, holding her breath, she watched his face. Watched him smile and reach out his arms as the nurse picked up the tiny, perfect bundle that was Callie.

Her daughter. *Their* daughter.

"Daddy would just love to hold his baby girl," Daniel said softly.

\* \* \* \* \*

*Fall in Love with...*

# MEN
# *in* UNIFORM

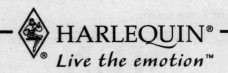

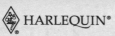

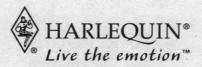

# HARLEQUIN®
# INTRIGUE®

## BREATHTAKING ROMANTIC SUSPENSE

Shared dangers and passions lead to electrifying
romance and heart-stopping suspense!

Every month, you'll meet six new heroes
who are guaranteed to make your spine tingle
and your pulse pound. With them you'll enter
into the exciting world of Harlequin Intrigue—
where your life is on the line
and so is your heart!

## THAT'S INTRIGUE—
## ROMANTIC SUSPENSE
## AT ITS BEST!

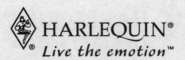

**HARLEQUIN®**
*Live the emotion™*

## HARLEQUIN® *Presents*

**The world's bestselling romance series...**
**The series that brings you your favorite authors,**
**month after month:**

Helen Bianchin...Emma Darcy
Lynne Graham...Penny Jordan
Miranda Lee...Sandra Marton
Anne Mather...Carole Mortimer
Melanie Milburne...Michelle Reid

**and many more talented authors!**

Wealthy, powerful, gorgeous men...
Women who have feelings just like your own...
The stories you love, set in exotic, glamorous locations...

## HARLEQUIN® *Presents*

**Seduction and Passion Guaranteed!**

www.eHarlequin.com

# HARLEQUIN®
# *Super Romance*®

# ...there's more to the story!

Superromance.
A *big* satisfying read about unforgettable
characters. Each month we offer *six* very different
stories that range from family drama to adventure
and mystery, from highly emotional stories to
romantic comedies—and much more! Stories
about people you'll believe in and care about.
Stories too compelling to put down....

Our authors are among today's *best* romance
writers. You'll find familiar names and talented
newcomers. Many of them are award winners—
and you'll see why!

If you want the biggest and best
in romance fiction, you'll get it
from Superromance!

## Exciting, Emotional, Unexpected...

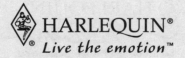

# HARLEQUIN®
*Live the emotion*™

## Harlequin® Historical
Historical Romantic Adventure!

*Imagine a time of chivalrous knights and unconventional ladies, roguish rakes and impetuous heiresses, rugged cowboys and spirited frontierswomen— these rich and vivid tales will capture your imagination!*

*Harlequin Historical... they're too good to miss!*

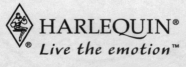